Die Once More

A Die for Me Novella

AMY PLUM

Interior Design by Woven Red Author Services, www.WovenRed.ca

Die for Her/Amy Plum—1st edition
ISBN ebook: 978-0-06-237975-7
ISBN print book: 978-2-9575891-1-1

Also by Amy Plum

The Die for Me Series
Die for Me
Until I Die
If I Should Die
Die for Her
Die Once More
Inside the World of Die for Me

After the End
Until the Beginning
(a duology)

Dreamfall
Neverwake
(a duology)

Chapter One

A new city. A new land. A new life. Or so I had hoped.

I left my friends, my country, the home I've had for a hundred years to escape a girl who has seen only seventeen summers. I put an ocean's distance between us just to discover it wasn't far enough.

We traded places: She's now in Paris, and I'm in New York. And therein is the problem. This is Kate's town, and it's like she never left. She's still here. She is everywhere.

In a week of walking the city streets, I feel like I've seen her a hundred times. From the American accents of high school girls chatting loudly on the subway to the downtown teenagers wearing her uniform of T-shirt, slim jeans, and Converses. She is in all of them, peering out of their eyes, taunting me with a love I will never taste. Because her heart is with another—my best friend, Vincent. I love him like a brother, but right now couldn't be gladder about the four thousand miles of ocean between us.

I wrap my coat tighter around me and lean out over my rooftop vantage point. Below me, chunks of floating ice turn the East River into one of the frozen martinis that seem to be endlessly flowing at my New York kindred's parties. For a bitingly cold daybreak the first week of March, the Paris sky would be spread with a blanket of gray clouds. But here in Brooklyn, where the sun has just risen, the sky is a dazzling field of cornflowers. The diamonds it casts on the surface of the water blind me. Bring me to tears. Or at least, provide a good excuse for my stinging eyes.

I hear a whistle, and turn to see my kindred Faust waiting for me next to a door shaft sticking up like a lone tombstone in the middle of the football-field-size roof. I make my way toward him, passing the barbecue pits and the giant swimming pool: all covered and hibernating. Waiting for the ice to melt and the city to move the party back outside again. The endless party. Life's a party in New York.

What am I doing here? I ask myself for the hundredth time. *Surviving,* is the correct response. *The only way I know how.*

"Council's ready for you," Faust says, clapping me across the shoulder as he guides me down the stairs.

"So I don't get it," he says. "You and your kindred come to New York a week ago on a mission to re-embody your kindred Vincent. You succeed, he goes back with the others, but you decide to hang out here at Frank and Myra's house. Then Vincent calls you to Paris, and after barely twenty-four hours in France you're back in New York?"

"What can I say? They were up against Violette and her army," I say, avoiding his point.

Faust nods. "Yeah, I guess you can't turn down a request from your kindred to help out with Paris's final battle against the numa. Man, what I would have given to be there and watch the Champion kick numa ass."

"It was a spur-of-the-moment thing," I respond. "Only room for twelve on Gold's plane. I would have brought more of you if I had understood what was going down."

"Frank and Myra . . . they're still in Paris, right?" Faust asks, eyes sparkling with good-natured jealousy. "I can't understand why you came back last night and didn't stick around for the after-party," he says, and then, seeing my blank expression, shuts up.

After a few seconds, he murmurs, "Man, we could sure use your Champion here. We've got our own bad stuff going down. But I'm sure you've heard all about that."

I follow him down six long flights of stairs. This building is massive, taking up a whole city block. Faust explains the floor plan as we descend.

"So you've already seen the roof. Next floor down, the seventh floor, is exhibition space, concert hall, and—as you probably saw last night—party headquarters. It's the only floor allowed to humans. That's why it has a dedicated elevator and stairway that don't access the other levels."

Faust points to a wall where industrial-size elevator cars are caged in by retracting metal gates. "Those go down to the basement. Man, you have to see that. It's so huge, there are actually two antique railroad tracks down there—used to bring goods in and out. At the front of the building we have river access for boats, and a dozen ambulances. The armory's down there too. Basically everything that's high security, and the stuff we don't want people to see, is belowground."

We exit the stairwell on the ground floor and begin making our way down the cavernous stone-gray corridors toward the front of the building. As we walk, I try to get a reading on Faust. He's got this regimented air, but not as much as a soldier or policeman. And he struts straight-backed, but with his arms slightly spread, like his muscles are getting in the way. He's already built big but has doubled his size with some serious time in the gym. Like most guys I've seen here, he favors facial hair: long razor stubble for him. Taking a wild guess, I would peg him as a fireman. I wonder if that's what he was before he died.

"So I've given you the layout. Now let me explain what it's all about," Faust says, switching into tour guide mode. "The building's a New York landmark, built of reinforced concrete in 1913 for a food processing company and then abandoned in the fifties."

I nod, and he continues. "Gold scooped it up for a song and made it our secret headquarters. No one realized we were operating out of here until the nineties . . . at which point it was decided to make it an open secret."

We turn a corner, and I begin to hear voices echoing through the cavernous corridors. "To the community, we're a bunch of artists, musicians, and young independent businesspeople— creative types—who've been granted these luxury living and working spaces by an arts foundation. We 'give back to the community' by opening the place up for exhibitions, concerts, and the monthly intel-gathering 'block parties' like we had last night."

He smiles at the memory of the epic party on the top floor of the building that just ended a few hours ago. It was in full swing when I arrived from the airport. I passed through, grabbed a drink, and spent the rest of the evening alone on the roof, until, after dawn, I saw the fleet of revenant-driven taxis shuttle the last partygoers home.

No partying for me. Not last night. Not with the gore of battle still fresh in my mind. Not after witnessing the permanent death of Jean-Baptiste, our leader. And in the midst of it all, my lovely Kate, fierce and beautiful and no longer human. I needed time to process it. To remember. To heal.

"It's the best spy network ever," Faust explains, jerking me back into the here and now. "The locals offer us up valuable information on our enemies without even knowing what they're giving us. The council always meets immediately after to discuss what we learned. So—perfect timing for your official welcome."Faust and I turn a corner and are in an airy, sunlit space occupying the entire front section of the building, overlooking the waterfront. A kitchen that could easily provide for several restaurants is fitted along the wall at the back. And between it and the floor-to-ceiling windows is a café area with around fifty tables. These are artfully grouped around potted trees strung with Christmas lights.

"This is where I leave you," Faust says, gesturing toward a gathering of ten tables arranged in a large circle. Several dozen of my New York kindred are seated there, waiting for me in a solemn silence. I move to stand behind the one empty chair left at the "head" of the circle—the one with the prime view of the river.

A familiar figure, dressed all in white, stands at the far end of the table to greet me. "Bardia of the five boroughs of New York, I present to you Jules Marchenoir, longtime Paris kindred," says Theodore Gold. "Witness for yourselves: His aura confirms him as one of us. Having met him before, I personally vouch for his goodwill, and I know that he is highly esteemed by the kindred of his birthplace."

"And *I* personally vouch for this man's ability to seduce half the human population of London without even breaking a sweat," interrupts a muscle-bound guy who could be Ambrose's older brother, drawing laughs from around the table. He holds up a fist, which I bump with my own as I take my seat next to him. "Met you at the '97 London convocation. Coleman Bailey, Harlem Riots of '43," he says, repeating a tradition I'd noticed with American revenants: introducing themselves with a detail of their death.

Gold chuckles, taking his seat, and says, "Sorry for the formal tone, Jules. There's a formula for introducing out-of-town revenants to kindred. Besides having a high number of immigrants, Americans also tend to move around a lot."

I nod and accept a glass and pitcher of water from the man sitting on my left. "We're used to formalities in the Old World," I say, trying my best to sound light. This is the last place I want to be: in the hot seat, having to explain myself to a lot of strangers while my brain is melting and my heart is in tiny jagged pieces—in a language that is not my own. But it's a necessary evil. If I want to stay, they need to know why.

My face has given something away: I see compassion on my kindred's faces. One girl speaks up. "We were so sorry to hear about Jean-Baptiste," she says, and everyone else nods and adds their own words of condolence.

Gold speaks up. "We're going to make this brief, Jules. No formal inquisition necessary. In America we don't have leaders or 'heads' like you do in Europe. Everything is done democratically. I usually speak for the crowd, since I am the official American historian—somewhat like Gaspard is for you. But any New York revenant animated over twenty years can be on the council, and it holds all the power."

Gold pauses and looks around the group, waiting to see if anyone wants to jump in. When no one does, he says, "You have expressed a desire to join us here in New York. Could you give us an indication of how long you plan on staying?"

Here we go. "An indeterminate amount of time, if you are willing to host me," I respond.

I see curiosity burn behind the eyes of the bardia. A member of the council speaks up. "Can you tell us the purpose of your stay?"

"I need time away from Paris," I say.

"Wouldn't your kindred prefer you to stay closer . . . say,

elsewhere in France?" she presses.

"At the moment, I was hoping for a bit more . . . distance." This is harder than I thought. If I could say it in French, I could add the innuendos needed to imply that it was a personal issue and they could mind their own damn business. But their expressions show openness and willingness to help me, so I swallow my bitterness. Note to self: They're not the ones I'm upset with.

"Your kindred called you back to France to fight with them barely two days ago," someone says, "and you complied. But you returned to New York last night—immediately after the battle. Can we conclude that this break from France is your decision, and not something wished for by your leaders?"

I take a moment to formulate my response. "My kindred would prefer that I stay. It is my decision to leave. But I am here with their blessing."

"We will not be perceived as taking your side in any type of personal dispute, then, if we welcome you among us?"

"Definitely not," I respond.

Everyone seems to relax. So this is what they were digging for.

Another man speaks up. "Thank you for the clarification. Jean-Baptiste named Vincent the head of France's revenants the same day you defected. We were worried about becoming involved in a power struggle."

I shake my head. "Vincent is the best man for that job. I support him fully." They are awaiting further explanation, but I'm not going to give them any. I'm not about to announce that I'm here because I'm heartbroken. That the woman I love is in love with my best friend. That it will kill me if I have to see them together any longer.

Around the table significant looks are being thrown among council members, and there is a general nodding of heads. A man with a mustache and a strong Southern accent speaks up. I have to listen closely to understand him. "Frederick Mackenzie, American Civil War. I'm acting administrator of the Warehouse. So far, you've been staying in the Greenpoint house. Gold says he put you there temporarily, since you knew Frank and Myra from a convocation. But we ask all newcomers to the New York clan—whether you're freshly animated or an old-timer from out of town—to live here in headquarters for the first six months. That way you can learn our ways without being an unwitting security risk just because you did things differently back home. After the six months, you are welcome to join a house in the borough of your choice, or, like many of our more sociable kindred, decide to stay here."

He pauses, and I nod to show I understand.

"Pre-council kindred often serve as welcome reps. Faustino, who you have already met, has been assigned to you. He'll be happy to show you around, explain the rules, and fix you up with your basic needs. Is there anything else we can do to make your transition to America easier?"

I'm not sure what to say. They're so . . . efficient.

A woman sitting next to Gold jumps in. "For those of you who don't already know of him, Jules Marchenoir is an accomplished artist. Perhaps those involved in the visual arts could provide him with necessary supplies, get him set up with a studio, and tell him when the life drawing group meets."

The woman is stunning—in an exotic kind of way: long black hair, copper-colored skin, almond eyes, and high cheekbones. I rack my brain but am sure I haven't seen her before. I would have remembered. So how does she know me?

"Thank you," I acknowledge gratefully.

She nods, but frowns, like the interaction is distasteful to her. Like I've offended her.

How bizarre. I must have met her before—it had to have been at a convocation. Did I try to pick her up or something? I doubt it—I restrict true flirting to human girls for just this reason. Why risk offending someone who could hold a grudge for eternity? Not to mention the danger of them falling in love. And who wants that?

Or at least that's how I used to think. Pre-Kate. She changed my game. Now I'd give up all the flirtations in the world just to be with her. Something pings sorely in my chest, and without thinking, I raise my hand to press it, drawing concerned looks. My kindred think I'm mourning. Let them. I am.

Gold breaks the silence. "Anyone else have a question?" He peers around the table. "No? Well, then I'll speak for all of us to say, 'Welcome, kindred.' We're glad you're here, Jules Marchenoir."

"Welcome!" several say together, like a cheer. People rise to go, several crowding around me to introduce themselves. Several ask about the French Champion—Kate. They want to know more details about how she emerged, and it is quickly obvious that their own numa problem is beginning to approach what we experienced in France.

My gaze drifts across the table to the girl who spoke earlier. A group of people stand around her, and the face that was stony with me is now radiant as she speaks with them.

A beautiful girl. Normally that would draw me like a moth to flame. Even with my no-kindred-lovers rule, a bit of playful banter and a shower of compliments (and the enjoyment of her inevitable response) would do my spirits a world of good. But not now. I don't even have it in me to say hello.

Her eyes lift and meet mine, and the coldness is like an ice ray. *What?* I ask her silently, shrugging my confusion.

She rolls her eyes—actually *rolls her eyes!*—and turns her

attention back to the person she's talking to.

Disconcerted, I look back to a man standing with his hand out and remember that I'm supposed to shake. No *bises*—cheek kisses—of course.

Faust appears and stands by my side as the room empties. "Need anything?" he whispers to me.

"Yes," I whisper back. "I would give my immortal soul to get out of here and walk."

Chapter Two

"The walk schedule is on the fridge," Faust says, once the last person has welcomed me. "This way." He leads me toward the kitchen.

"A schedule?" I ask.

"Does that surprise you?" he asks, flashing a curious smile.

"I'm not sure what's more surprising, that there's a schedule or that it's being displayed on something as banal as a refrigerator," I admit.

Faust laughs. "There are about two hundred bardia in the five boroughs. Everybody has their own room here, but about half choose to live elsewhere, and they usually walk with their houses in their own neighborhoods. That leaves about a hundred of us here. A schedule's pretty much necessary."

"And the fridge?" I ask.

He grins. "Where did everyone hang out in your house in Paris?"

"In the kitchen," I concede.

We arrive at a row of three enormous refrigerators. Stuck to one is a printed schedule with names, days of the week, and neighborhoods. I whistle, impressed.

"We had it online for a while," Faust explains. "A couple of our tech-minded kindred even developed an app. But after our enemies hacked in a couple of times and showed up to meet us at our scheduled places, we went back to the old-fashioned paper-and-ink method."

"Is the numa presence strong here?" I ask.

"Getting worse all the time," Faust murmurs, running his finger down the chart. "Even starting to organize, as much as murderous immortals who are only out for themselves can do. Crime boss in our area is called Janus. But there are others . . . bigger fish that we're not even near catching.

"I'll tell you—all eyes were on Paris a couple days ago. Folks can't stop talking about your Champion. As in, we need her here. Stat."

I cringe inside. That's all I need: to play musical countries with Kate. If she comes here, there's no way I can stay.

Faust traces across a row of names and stops. "Let's see. Green team's got the sunrise shift. They're taking off in a few minutes and are covering Williamsburg and the surrounding area. It would be good for you to get to know our hood."

"Thanks," I say. "I really need this walk."

"Got the craving?" Faust asks with concern. "How long's it been?"

"Since I died? Only a few months."

"And you probably loaded up on dark energy from the numa-slaying extravaganza in Paris," he says, with the same wish-I'd-been-there look. Faust loves a fight, that much is obvious. He should team up with Ambrose—they'd be unstoppable.

I nod. "I killed six."

He whistles. "You should be good for a while, then. Just need the fresh air?" he jokes.

"Close," I say. "I could use the distraction."

~

I stand outside the loading dock, the meet-up point listed on the schedule, waiting for the "Green" team to appear. My hands shoved deep in my coat pockets, I bounce up and down, trying to generate a bit of heat, and try not to think about what my kindred are doing in Paris. Celebrating their victory with their new Champion. I get a flashback of Kate's face, not even two days ago in the midst of battle—streaked with blood and dirt and ash, glowing with the golden bardia aura. And though animating didn't seem to have changed her features, in my eyes she was more beautiful than ever.

My chest aches. How long will it take me to get over her? I am relieved when I hear footsteps crunch on the frost-frozen pavement behind me.

I turn. It's the girl from the council. The Frost Queen. *At least she's in her element,* I think, as my breath puffs out in a thick cloud.

"Marchenoir," she says in greeting, her face blank. Ice-cold. She's bundled up in a calf-length padded coat, and her long black hair cascades out from under an eggplant-colored slouchy knit cap.

I respond by giving her a full bend-at-the-waist, arm-thrown-to the side bow. "At your service." I can't help myself, unsure of whether I am trying to crack her facade or just annoy her in return for her iciness. Maybe both.

She ignores me and watches as Faust comes jogging up from behind us, rubbing his gloved hands up and down his arms for warmth. "I traded with Palmer," he says, and gives me a grin. "Don't want to shirk my 'welcome rep' responsibilities. Not that Whitefoot here couldn't show you the ropes." He gives her a playful punch on the arm, and she gives him a smile so warm I'm surprised it doesn't melt half the ice in New York.

How does she do it . . . arctic to tropical in a second flat? I would be impressed if I wasn't on the end of the stick reserved for polar bears.

With effort, Faust manages to pry his eyes away from her and hands me a leather belt with a holster on each side. "Two weapons?" I ask. He nods as I strap it around my waist. "Short-sword," he says, handing me the blade. I inspect it before slipping it into my belt: It's brand-new, unlike the antique models we use in France, but well made. "And a Glock," he says, handing me a pistol.

I look up at him in surprise.

"It's enough, really. You don't really need an automatic," he explains, misunderstanding my expression. "We never come up against more than a few numa at a time. And even that's pretty rare, unless we're zombie hunting. Today's just a regular walk around the block."

I glance at "Whitefoot." She's amused by my confusion. "Like it or not, guns are the American way. Shoot to the head to stun, then use your blade," she clarifies.

That's the way Lucien cut down Gaspard to get into La Maison, I remember. Gunshot to the head, then—while the projectile worked its way back out of Gaspard's bullet-rejecting flesh—decapitation by sword. American way, huh? I wonder if Lucien made any trips to the States before meeting his end at the tip of Kate's blade.

I holster the gun and pull the sides of my long wool coat over the weapons to hide them. The Frost Queen, "Frosty," I decide to christen her since I still don't know her first name, has already turned and is walking away. She points up and says, "We've got your old colleagues with us, Faust." And then, speaking to the air, she says, "Ryan, you go with Marchenoir, Tirado's with Faust, and I've got Oreo. Let's move it out."

"Three volant spirits?" I ask.

Faust shrugs. "More of the American way, I guess."

Okay. Guns. One volant per walking revenant. I can accept that. It's the minor cultural differences that throw me more. Like the last name/nickname thing: It's more like army-speak than talk among kindred. Though there's no way two hundred bardia in one city could be as closely knit as our much smaller Paris crowd. Which, at the moment, is exactly how I like it. Arm's length sounds pretty good to me.

We begin walking away from the river, into the central part of the Brooklyn neighborhood called Williamsburg. The voice of the volant spirit assigned to me appears in my mind. *Hey Frenchie. Anthony Ryan here, Ground Zero. I've got your back.*

"Hi," I respond, and I hear Frosty and Faust check in with their invisible partners. Ghostly communication only works one way. They can get inside our heads—but we can't get into theirs. "You can call me Jules."

Okay, Frenchie, the voice responds.

Frosty starts giving orders. "Ryan, head north toward Greenpoint. Tirado straight ahead toward Bushwick Avenue. And Oreo, sweep over toward Bed-Stuy and the Navy Yard. Start within a twenty-minute walk of our location, and then sweep back toward us." I feel the volant spirits leave us, and it's once again three dead guys—make that two dead guys and a girl—walking the streets in the frigid morning air.

Faust points things out as we go: the main street, called Bedford. The fact that this neighborhood has boomed in the last few decades, luxury apartments and wealthy tenants replacing the Polish and Italian immigrants in one part, European Jewish and Hispanic populations in another. We walk by brand-new bars and restaurants and pass hipster guys with tight jeans and beards and girls with tattoos and thick, winged eyeliner.

The changes have made things easier for the bardia. When the neighborhood was made up of families who stayed for generations, caution was an everyday concern. But with people constantly moving in and out, they don't have to worry about hiding faces that never change.

I remember my volant spirit's introduction. "What's Ground Zero mean?" I ask.

"What about Ground Zero?" Faust asks.

"That's how Ryan introduced himself," I clarify.

Faust answers, "Ground Zero. Twin Towers. September eleventh ..." and before he even finishes, I get it. "*Onze septembre*," I translate, "of course. Ryan was there?"

"We all were," he responds, "most of us pre-council newbies you'll meet at the Warehouse. More bardia made that day than in the entire history of New York City." His face darkens. "And a few numa too."

We turn, heading toward the Williamsburg Bridge, and follow it away from the river. Frosty walks a few paces in front of us, but I can tell she's listening to every word.

"We heard all about it in France," I say, and think about the ramifications of what Faust just told me. "But the dead were so high profile! There were leaflets with your faces all over the place. How were you even able to stay in the New York area after animating?"

"Gold made sure those of us he recovered were certified dead and taken off the search lists. Those who had families or communities who might recognize them were moved farther away. Ryan, Tirado, Oreo, and me ... we all decided to stay. My parents are dead, but I have a little sister I like to keep an eye on. I visit her when I'm volant." He's quiet, studying the ground in front of his feet.

It's got to be hard for him. He still has surviving family members he can't show himself to. Everyone I knew before I animated has been dead for generations.

As if reading my mind, Faust glances up at me. "At least I get to do what I love: save lives. Never thought I'd be signing up for an eternal contract when I became a firefighter . . ."

Called it! I think. A century of watching people has paid off once again.

". . . but I can't think of a better reason to exist."

Frosty slows, puts an arm around Faust's shoulder, and gives him a sideways hug. "One of New York's finest," she says, and astounds me once again by giving him a peck on the cheek. He gives her a sad smile and then abruptly looks up, listening.

"Tirado's got something over on Bushwick and Devoe. Three of our evil twins . . . on their way to stir up trouble, no doubt."

"At this time in the morning?" I ask, as the three of us jog in the direction he had pointed.

"New York: the city that never sleeps," quotes Faust.

Frosty fills me in as she runs. "We wondered if news of your battle in Paris had reached our city's numa, and if so, if they would react. If it would make any difference to them. Their activity's been growing steadily over the last decade, but recently something . . . different . . . seems to have been brewing," she says, confirming what Faust said.

She throws a glance at me, a flicker of worry flashing across her blank-screen face, and says cryptically, "The dark prophecy that gave you your Champion doesn't only refer to France. It's the Third Age here too, you know."

Chapter Three

We arrive at a four-story box-shaped building that looks like it's been sided with roof tiles. Green. Ugly. I shouldn't care, but used to the beauty of Paris, I can't help but cringe. It looks like an architect threw up on a blueprint and decided it looked good that way.

I'm back, Frenchie. Miss me? Ryan says in my head. I see Faust and Frosty talking to the air and know the volant spirits have congregated. "What do you see?" I ask him.

Top-floor apartment, he responds. *Three numa versus four trust-fund-looking twentysomethings.* His voice disappears for a moment, and then he's back. *The kids are selling drugs for the zombies and didn't turn over all the money. Typical TV cop-series scenario. Could have written a better script myself. Oh great . . . here come the numa volants.*

Frosty talks to her spirit for another moment and then announces, "Okay, we're on our own. The numa brought a volant each, and they're blocking ours. I've sent Oreo back to the Warehouse for reinforcements. Ryan and Tirado, do what you can to stay with us."

She turns from where she's staring into space and focuses on Faust and me. What'd you get from your volants?"

"Three numa, four twentysomething kids shifting drugs for them, deal gone bad," Faust summarizes, fingering his weapons and looking up at the building.

"Same for me," I say, "and Ryan specified top floor."

"Oreo got more," she says. "A numa forced one of the kids to overdose. Got the opioid injection?" she asks Faust. He nods. "We have two entries: one through the front door and the other at the back through a fire escape. Faust, go up that way and block the exit." Faust takes off around the side of the building. "Wait for my signal, and then enter if you can without breaking the window," Frosty calls after him. He waves to show he heard her.

She marches up the front steps, her long quilted coat flying open on either side as she unbuttons it, fishes around in the pockets, and pulls out a large set of keys. Leaning over to inspect the lock on the front door, she murmurs, "Schlage single cylinder," and rifles through the key collection. Sticking one in the lock, she turns it and opens the door. I follow her into a small front-hall area with another locked door in front of us. Boxes and letters are stacked haphazardly on a side table.

Without hesitating, Frosty picks up a large Amazon box, inspects it, rings a doorbell labeled APT 1, and when a voice asks, "Yes?" she says, "FedEx." The door buzzes open, she heaves the box toward a door marked 1, and we're off, running noiselessly up the stairs.

From behind us I hear a door open, the shuffle of someone dragging the box into their apartment, and then the door closing. *Good trick,* I think with awe, understanding now why New York bardia insist on training out-of-towners in their ways before letting them loose. The simple technique of getting into a locked building without drawing unwanted attention would never have occurred to me. I can get into any building in Paris but would be totally lost here.

We get to the top floor, and Frosty pauses by the door, pressing her ear carefully to it, before slowly turning the door handle, testing. It's unlocked.

I follow her lead as she draws only her gun, leaving her sword hidden beneath her coat. The Glock feels bulky in my hand, its screwed-on silencer weighing down the already heavy weapon. I haven't held one of these since Ambrose, Vincent, and I posed as undercover security forces for a Paris embassy during the Gulf War.

"Take whoever's near the door," she whispers to me, and then, putting her fingers between her lips, lets out an ear-piercing whistle and shoves the door open, landing a forceful blow to whoever was behind it.

We're in a short hallway. The open door blocks the access to the rear of the apartment, leaving whoever's behind it for Faust to handle. We turn left and find ourselves in a chaotic living room, broken furniture tossed around, and drawn curtains blocking the morning light. Two young men and a woman huddle, crying, on a couch while two imposing numa, outlined in bloodred auras, loom over them, one pointing a gun at their captives. Another man is slumped over on the floor at their feet, eyes open, but obviously unconscious . . . if not already dead.

I take all this in at a glance, while from behind the door I hear the thick thud of a silenced gunshot, and Faust calls, "One down."

Before his words are out, Frosty has put a bullet in the numa holding the gun, and he collapses. Rushing past her, I press my gun to the remaining numa's temple as he reaches for his weapon. He drops his pistol and holds his hands up.

"Quickly," Frosty says to the kids on the couch. "Take cover in the bathroom, and lock the door behind you."

She doesn't need to say it twice. In a second, they're up and scrambling for a door across the room. They disappear behind it, I hear a lock turn from the inside, and then dead silence.

"What are you doing here?" Frosty steps over the numa she downed and strolls over to us.

My numa tenses, and I press the barrel tighter to his head.

"What's it look like? Business," he mutters.

"Whose business? Janus's?" she asks.

He narrows his eyes at her and nods.

"So he dares to send his muscle a mere ten blocks away from our headquarters, just to put some scare into a bunch of stupid kids? Business must be booming."

The guy just glares at her.

"You're in our neighborhood, eight in the morning, full daylight. Know what that tells me about you and your friends?" she asks.

The man looks like he's thinking it over, but before he can come to a conclusion, she points her own gun right between his eyes. "It tells me you're expendable," she says, and pulls the trigger.

As the man crumples, behind me I hear a clink of metal against wood. I turn to see the numa Frosty shot first flex his fingers, as the bullet that has worked its way out of his flesh rolls around on the floor inches from his forehead. He begins pushing himself up from where he lies in a small pool of blood.

"Blades," Frosty says, and the three of us draw our swords, Faust and his fallen numa just visible in the hallway behind the open doorway. There is a second of silence as we hold them high, then, together, bring them down.

"Deliver us from evil," Faust murmurs, crossing himself, as he nudges the numa head away with his foot and closes the door behind him. As the surge of dark energy hits us, I see Faust clench his fists and take it like a shot of adrenaline. Frosty closes her eyes and breathes in deeply, storing hers up. I shudder as mine floods me. The big reward for killing numa: We get their energy when they die. And we also gift the world with one less bad guy. It's a win-win situation.

"Treat the overdose," Frosty calls to Faust, and he moves quickly to care for the unconscious boy. She turns to me. "Go downstairs and let our backups in," she orders.

As I leave, I see her go over to the bathroom door and knock. "Is everyone okay in there?" she asks. Muffled affirmations come from behind the door. "Just stay where you are for the moment. Sit tight. You're all going to be okay."

Her voice is firm and reassuring, but as she turns away and my eye catches hers, I know she is telling a half-truth. These kids got out of this scene alive, but they're already chin-deep in numa business. It's going to take a lot of intervention on our part, if they'll even accept our help, for them to truly be okay.

Frosty knows how things work here. She's been around for a while, but not too long. I can tell from her aura . . . from her eyes . . . that she's a much younger revenant than I. But the power I see in her leaves no question of her nature in my mind. She is trying to appear normal, chummy with her kindred, on equal terms with the others. But I'm from a place where hierarchy has reigned for centuries . . . millennia even. True leaders have come and gone: I've read about them in Gaspard's records, and met a few at convocations. And I know without a doubt that this woman was born to be among them. Born to be a queen. Forget Ice Queen, Frost Queen. I'm in the presence of a girl who has the potential to be the Queen . . . of New York.

Chapter Four

Two months creep by, and things do not get better. Every day is like its own separate death, bullet-riddled with memories and gutted by the twisting knife of loss. Entwined with the memories of Kate, and the longing for a love that will never be, is the loss of my best friend. My mood swings wildly between missing the camaraderie of a brother I had for over seventy years, and resenting him for being the recipient of Kate's love.

And then there's Jean-Baptiste. Although I was never as close to him as Vincent was, I loved and respected the man. I should be there to help support Gaspard in his grief. So there's that guilt to deal with, along with all the rest.

Losing Vincent is like losing my right arm. And since Kate has my heart, and I feel spineless for abandoning Gaspard, you could say I'm presently suffering a major lack of body parts.

The only way I survive is to never stop moving. I make sure I'm always surrounded by others, so I won't have time to think and end up imploding like a dying star.

I walk incessantly. I know the streets of Brooklyn and Manhattan, my two chosen boroughs, well enough by now to have an accurate street map in my head. I sign up for three four-hour shifts per day. Although that first day was an exception, and New York's numa are staying suspiciously out of sight, there are enough cases of suffering street people, suicide attempts, domestic violence, and near-fatal accidents to keep me on a continual high from the life force I absorb from these saves.

"Dude, this isn't a contest," Faust says as I trim my hair in my studio mirror. "You don't get bonus points if you save more humans than anyone else."

He has been an impeccable welcome rep. He got me moved into my room at the Warehouse and had it furnished with what I asked for. (I didn't really care, but he pushed me for details until it ended up looking pretty much exactly like my room in Paris . . . besides the floor-to-ceiling windows with an enviable view of the East River.) He got me weather-appropriate clothes, made sure the armory had what I needed (sending off for some antique swords so I would "feel at home"), and introduced me to our kindred artists—of whom there are many. Seems like every revenant artist in America wants to be here.

Faust even gamely accompanied me to my first Midnight Drawing Group meeting at the Warehouse. But after Gina, one of our bardia sisters recruited to pose when our human model didn't show up, perched atop the stool and dropped her robe, Faust's jaw dropped too. Her response was, "Draw or scram, Faust." He hasn't been back since. His third-generation Italian-American upbringing and his stint in the tough-guy New York fire department never prepared him for people like the artists I hang out with.

It was Gina, drawing next to me one night, who first pointed out that the girl I was sketching looked nothing like the model posing for us on the stool. I didn't respond—what could I say? Since then no one else has mentioned the fact that every woman I draw is the same. The position matches that of our model, the shadows and light are exactly what they are in our studio, but it is always Kate's face, always her body. My pencil has its own will, and my fingers are its slaves.

Late one evening, Gold drops by with a message from Paris. He takes one look at the girl on my drawing pad, and I see things click in his mind. Tearing his eyes from the page, he says, "I have something for you." He waves a creamy white envelope like a flag.

As I reach for it, he slips it back into his pocket and says, "I'd actually been hoping to catch up with you." He glances around at the twenty-odd people concentrating on their drawings. "Without disrupting everyone, of course. Do you have time for a break?"

I fold up my sketchbook and, tucking it under my arm, lead him down one floor and to my room. "Tea?" I ask, as he peruses my space, inspecting the paintings and drawings that have accumulated in stacks around the walls and on every available surface. Many show the humans I've saved in the past few weeks. The others, well . . .

"With milk," he responds, and picks up a small portrait of a girl with her arms crossed. I painted it in the style of my old friend Modigliani, kind of an homage to his girlfriend Jeanne. But instead of Jeanne staring doe-like from the canvas, Kate's laughing eyes gaze out, and the expression of wry amusement she makes when I tease her curves one corner of her lips.

"This is why," states Gold, as I set a steaming cup on a table near him and pull a jug of milk from the mini-fridge.

"Why what?" I ask, knowing exactly what he's talking about.

"Why you stayed. Why over the last two and a half months you've been acting like an overachieving Superman who can't stop rescuing people long enough to breathe. Or in your case, long enough to remember."

"Do you double as the house shrink?" I ask, lifting my own mug to my lips and blowing off a cloud of jasmine-scented steam.

"I try to avoid that at all costs, actually," Gold says, chuckling, and glances back down at the painting. "No one here knows what's wrong with you. You haven't confided in any of your kindred. Not even Faust, and that boy's practically spent twenty-four/seven with you."

"So the welcome reps serve as your spies?" I say, immediately regretting it. Faust has been more than welcoming. He's been a friend. He's tried to crack my shell, but I'm not letting anyone in. They wouldn't want to see the mess inside.

Whatever Gold sees in my face allows him to forgive my rude comment and change the subject. "I suppose this means you won't be going to Paris for the wedding?" He hands me the ivory envelope, and, thrusting his hands into his pockets, walks to the window. He looks out over the ink-black river toward the hushed lights of the city.

I set my tea down and pull out a creamy card engraved in silvery-blue ink.

Charlotte Violaine Lorieux et Ambrose Bates
ont la joie de vous faire part de leur mariage
le samedi 28 mai
A l'église de la Sainte-Chapelle, Paris

So Ambrose and Charlotte are getting married—I check the date—exactly three months after our epic battle with the numa. The battle Ambrose had to miss because of a wound suffered in a skirmish, just hours before. And the battle where I helped Kate drag Charlotte's dead body to the side of the arena so that it wouldn't be scooped up by numa and burned.

I knew, of course, of their newly kindled love. Gaspard has sent me one letter per week—handwritten and mailed through the post—updating me on the goings-on of the Paris kindred.

And Ambrose phoned me once on the cell phone I was issued by my new kindred. He told me he had proposed. That Charlotte had accepted. Of course. Any idiot except Ambrose would have known she's been in love with him for decades. But for Ambrose this love was a revelation, and the more he talked about it, the wider the pit inside me grew, its emptiness swallowing all my words until finally he just told me he loved me and that they all missed me, and he hung up.

I never wanted love. Until Kate. And now it eats at me from inside, reminding me of how stupid I've been. How shallow. All that time wasted, when I could have been happy like Ambrose and Charlotte. Like Vincent and Kate. But what if Kate was the one? She's the only girl who has ever made me long for permanence. What if she was the one, and I could have done more to let her know? What if I had been honest sooner?

No, she and Vincent were made for each other. That much is clear. I'm just cursed to want what is not meant to be. But damn my heart for switching on—finally—for the wrong person. Now it is an open door, standing wide for nothing . . . for no one . . . and I don't know how to close it again.

I look up and see that Gold is waiting for a response. "Um, no. I don't really think I'll make it to the wedding. Too soon. And I've got my work here."

"Wrong answer," says Gold. He looks back out the window at his city, before ambling back to me, authority radiating from him. This is his world, and has been for more than a century. I'm just a blip on his radar. Passing through.

"We need you to go."

"What?" I exclaim. "What's that supposed to mean? If *you*

want to go to the wedding, I'm sure the bride and groom wouldn't mind if you took my place."

Gold looks back at me, the picture of patience. "When you joined us, you agreed to work for the good of the clan. No one can deny the fact that you've been doing more than your share of patrolling. But we have other jobs that need to be done, and in this case, you're the one to do it."

Chapter Five

I stand frozen in disbelief while Gold picks up my jacket and throws it at me. "Here, let's walk, and I'll explain along the way." He plucks the invitation from my hand and pockets it, while I reach to grab my weapon belt.

"You won't need that," he says dismissively. "We're not patrolling."

"You never know," I say, and put it on anyway, slipping a short-sword into the holster before shrugging on the leather jacket, which is cut long enough to hide steel. I leave my gun on the table. I carry it when I need to but don't enjoy how it feels: There's something dead about it, unlike the almost-living vibration a sword emits.

We walk out of the Warehouse into a breezy May night, the midnight moon scattering disks of gold on the surface of the wind-rippled water. Heading away from the river toward the center of Williamsburg, we move away from the glass-covered high-rises into a neighborhood of three-story brownstones.

While we walk, Gold fills me in on the recent history of New York's revenants. I have the feeling he's just passing time so that I won't press him for details on this special mission, but his words catch my attention, and I let him spin the tale in his old-fashioned roundabout way.

"In the sixties and seventies," he says, hands thrust into his pockets as he digs back in his memory, "New York's numa were out of control. Violence was at a high, and anarchy reigned. The city was the undisputed murder capital of America. That's when we bardia decided to reorganize, and instead of continuing our traditional role in the city—that of saving humans on an individual basis—we decided to infiltrate the system. During the next decade, we focused on placing bardia in roles of authority, both in the government and in the city's administration: police, fire, emergency services. Things started to turn around in the nineties.

"Of course, we never ran for office—didn't want the visibility. But today, behind each and every fire chief, police commissioner, councilman, and even mayor, there is significant bardia influence. Have you heard about a mayor called Giuliani, who 'single-handedly' cleaned up New York City during his eight years in office?"

I nod. "Even in France we heard of him."

Gold chuckles. "Some say he went too far. Took some of the city's character away along with its sex shops and illegal street vendors. Maybe so. But that entire initiative can be credited to a bardia named Tristan Fielding, a friend of mine from my human days. When we were alive, in the nineteenth century, the gangs of New York were terrorizing the Lower East Side. More than a hundred years later, some of the same numa who had been involved in that crime scene were still making trouble.

"While the New York administration cleaned up the human mess, we took out most of the numa population: either running them out of town or destroying them. And the balance swayed in our favor for a good ten years. Until September eleventh, 2001."

I can't help but shudder when he says that date. It's as if the numbers hold a dark power when spoken together. Pure evil. "Faust told me that more bardia were made on that day than any other in New York's history."

Gold nods. "We've got two seers here—me and Coleman Bailey, who sat next to you at the council meeting. The two of us kept busy for days and had the entire kindred working along with us. Too bad we can't see when numa are created. Could have destroyed them before they were even animated."

"I thought there were only a dozen or so hijackers. Don't tell me they animated after being incinerated in the tower fires!" I say.

"No, they were gone, as far as we can tell. But evil draws evil, and the slaughter of human lives that happened that day acted like a magnet for our enemies. But more importantly was the one behind it all. Most men who engineer mass killings have a core of evil in them that comes from somewhere subhuman. Whether numa himself or advised by numa, you can bet the architect of 9/11 had close links to our enemies."

"Are you talking about . . . ," I begin.

Gold looks around like he's worried someone's listening, although the street we're walking down is empty, and most houses we pass completely dark. "Why do you think there was no photo or DNA evidence of his death released to the public? Buried at sea? Right. After his head was chopped off and his body incinerated, perhaps. Gunshots aren't enough to kill a numa overlord. Our men in the Pentagon made sure he was good and gone and not rising from the grave three days later."

"Bardia in the Pentagon?" I ask, truly astounded.

"Like I said, our style here is to infiltrate and advise. Not just in New York, but all over America," Gold says with a grin.

I am speechless. I honestly had no idea. This country is a

millennium younger than ours, but man, do they know how to handle their own.

We turn onto a quiet side street, just one block long, nestled between two larger avenues. The brownstones here look homey, and the street is squeaky clean, like its inhabitants take pride in their hidden haven.

"All that is to say," Gold says, as we walk up a set of concrete steps to a green door with a big number 16 in brass letters in the middle, "the numa population has exploded here since 2001. Things seem to be coming to a head, and something has to be done. Something like what happened in Paris. That's why we need you to go there." Gold turns from me and rings the doorbell.

"But," I begin, and then I stop, because the door is opening and above us stands Frosty, in all her copper-skinned, raven-haired glory. I haven't seen her since the drug bust and have a feeling that that isn't a coincidence. I know she's been around—she's obviously been avoiding me.

Evidence: Her face lights up when she sees Gold, but when I step from the shadows behind him, out comes the permafrost.

"Ava, my dear, how good to see you," says Gold, and steps up to give her a good old American hug. So. Frosty Whitefoot has a first name. Trust old-fashioned Gold to fly in the face of current convention and use it.

He lets go of her and turns toward me. "You remember Jules Marchenoir," he says.

"Yes. We walked together his first week. Took down those numa on Bushwick," Ava says stiffly, putting her hands on her hips as she stares down at me.

"Oh yes, I had forgotten," says Gold. "May we come in?" Even he has noticed her reaction to me and is waiting, puzzled, for her to stop body-blocking the door and invite us in.

"Of course," she replies, shaking her head as if clearing a fog, and steps aside to let us pass. She shuts the door and double-bolts it before ushering us into a large room with mid-century minimalist couches arranged around an old-fashioned fireplace.

One of those dogs that looks like it has a full-on shaggy mustache lies on a rug in front of the chimney, and upon seeing us rolls onto its back to have its belly rubbed. Gold obliges, adjusting his white suit in order to squat down, and baby-talks to "Vera" as he proceeds to massage the blissed-out pooch into dog heaven.

Gold's obviously been here before—he doesn't give the room a second glance—but I am mesmerized by its contents. Art. Everywhere. I can't help myself: I have to look, and wander from picture to picture, inspecting them carefully. There are several examples of pop art by artists whose names sound vaguely familiar. A framed Velvet Underground poster hangs on one wall, signed, *To Ava, my one true love (among many), Lou* and under that, *Sisters in crime: Ava + Nico.* A Salvador Dali sketch stands framed on a table: a nude woman with a bouquet of flowers instead of a head, with the dedication, *To the divine Ava,* scrawled underneath.

And above the mantel is the pièce de résistance: a giant silkscreen of Ava's head by Warhol himself. In it, a patterned turban hides her hair, and her chin is raised as if in defiance. With her dark-copper skin, high cheekbones, and almond-shaped eyes, she looks like some sort of native warrior: but native to where, it's not clear.

"Who were you?" The words leave my lips before I can stop them.

"Doesn't matter," she says, and Gold looks up abruptly from the dog-fest. He looks as confounded by her brusqueness as I am.

"Ava was a part of Andy Warhol's Factory—she was his favorite for a couple of years," Gold says, before she shoots him a look that forbids him to spill more. "Now, of course, she is a well-respected art historian, specializing in American art of the sixties and seventies. Not much of an overlap with my own specialty of antiquities, of course, but we historians stick together."

He smiles up at her, breaking her stoniness enough to let a fond smile shine through. It's obvious: They aren't just kindred. They are friends.

Gold stands and straightens his suit. "Well, this isn't a social call, my dear, so let's get down to business. Jules was invited to the wedding of two of his Paris kindred. It's taking place in just under two weeks.

"On the way here, I explained the history behind the heightened numa presence in New York. I explained that we fear things coming to a head like they did in Paris, and that it might end in a deciding battle." It's obvious from the looks on both of their faces that this is a topic they have discussed at length. Gold is just letting Ava know how much he's told me. He crosses his arms, all business.

"I have spoken to some others, and we want you to accompany Jules to Paris, to gather as much information as you can from our French kindred about recent advances they've made, especially interviewing the *guérisseur*, Bran, as to anything that may give us an advantage in an upcoming struggle. If it is deemed necessary, you could make an official request in the name of the council that the Champion return to help us." A look passes between them. There's something they're not telling me. Probably a lot of things they're not telling me. But that's not what's bothering me at the moment.

"Listen, Gold. Why do you need me to go?" I say. "Why can't you accompany Ava to France? I'm not"—*ready*—"prepared to travel. I'm still assimilating to life in New York and would rather delay my return until I'm totally comfortable here." That's a load of crap, and both Ava and Gold know it, but it's all I can think of at the moment.

"I am needed here," Gold says. "Plus, it's your kindred and their *guérisseur* that we need to consult with. You are the natural choice for a liaison."

"We will need to be accompanied, of course," Ava says, a soupçon of alarm showing through her mask of self-control. She doesn't want to be alone with me. Once again, I wonder what I possibly could have done to offend this woman.

"Of course, three is always better even if no one is *volant*," Gold agrees. "It has been suggested that Faustino go with you. But let's limit the number. I don't want to make a big deal of it and possibly alert our enemies to our movements. This wedding is the perfect cover for our fact-finding mission."

Gold nods, like his job is now over. He looks back and forth between us. "Well?" he asks. "You better get your stuff together. I reserved your plane for six a.m. That gives you exactly"—he pulls his shirtsleeve back and inspects a large gold wristwatch—"two hours until you need to leave for JFK. I'd get packing if I were you."

"Two hours?" I exclaim. "Why the rush if you're chartering a plane?"

"Why wait?" Gold challenges. "Ava's got her work cut out for her. The more research she can do before our Paris kindred are completely distracted by wedding festivities, the better."

"Don't you think we ought to talk to Gaspard first?" I ask, my final plea to get out of this mess.

"Yes, of course," Gold says, and pulls a phone out of his pocket. He taps a button and holds it up to his ear. I hear Gaspard yell, "*Oui, allo?*" at his phone, and picture him holding it out at arm's distance like he always does.

"Gaspard, my dear, it's Theo. Everything's going according to plan: Ava and Jules, plus one of our kindred accompanying," Gold says, looking smug.

"They're coming!" I hear Gaspard yell in French on the other end, resulting in a scream that could only be Charlotte in freak-out mode. *Now there's no way of backing out,* I think, my heart dropping.

Gold turns away from us to continue the conversation with Gaspard, and I look toward Ava, who wears an expression of feigned boredom. "Is he always this pushy?" I ask.

Ava crosses her arms and rolls her eyes. "You have no idea."

Chapter Six

The plane trip is interminable. There are times when I wish revenants could sleep, and this is definitely one of them. Gold chartered a four-person jet, which would normally be sufficient, but the way things are going, I wish we were on a jumbo, with rows and rows of empty seats between us.

Once he got over the shock that he'd been tapped to go to Paris, Faust had just enough time to get his hands on a French guidebook, and began practicing phrases on me as soon as the plane took off.

We're two hours into the flight and he's still on, "*Où est la gare?*"

"Faust, you're not going to need a train station," I moan.

He nods and flips through to another page. "*Voulez-vous dîner avec moi ce soir?*"

"What is this?" I ask, and pluck the book out of his grasp. The chapter is entitled, "Relationships and Dating." I toss it back to him, and, leaning my head back against the headrest, wearily respond, "You're not going to pick up a French girl by asking her out to dinner. You've got to begin with compliments. Start with something safe: her eyes. Her smile."

I feel little darts of hatred piercing my skin, and turn to where Ava sits ensconced behind a laptop. She has been pointedly ignoring us the whole time, but now she's giving me a look of unadulterated disgust.

"What?" I ask, throwing my hands up in frustration. I don't understand what this woman's problem is with me.

She just shakes her head and goes back to typing. A pencil is tucked behind her ear, lending her appearance the slightest hint of naughty librarian. Interesting. *Stop it, Jules*, I chide. *This girl is dangerous.*

I look back to Faust, who has jotted down a note on the dating page, *Eyes. Smile.* He closes the book and taps it impatiently with his pencil.

"Speaking of smiling, I don't get why you're not supposed to smile in public," he said, leaning back in his seat, his hands folded behind his head, displaying triceps that rival Ambrose's.

"What are you talking about?" I ask.

"It's in the etiquette rules chapter," he says.

"Why on earth are you worried about French rules of etiquette?"

"It's my first time outside the United States, besides Mexico," he responds. "I want to do this right."

I sigh. "You'll probably be with kindred most of the time, but okay. What does it say?"

I reach for the book, but he puts a hand out to stop me. "No, no. I've got it memorized." He tips his head back, stares at the ceiling, and begins counting on his index. "One. When you go into a shop, say '*Bonjour, monsieur*' or '*Bonjour, madame*' as soon as you step through the door, and '*au revoir*' when you leave."

He glances over at me. I nod. "Common courtesy," I say.

He adds his middle finger. "Two. You're expected to order one drink per hour in a café—you can't just sit there all day on one drink."

"That's an approximation," I say, "but yeah, it's kind of like renting a table."

He nods, satisfied. "There are about ten others. They all pretty much made sense. Except for the smiling one. It said you're not supposed to walk around with a smile on your face, and I quote, 'American style.' What's up with that?"

"Okay, New Yorkers excepted, most Americans smile a lot more than the typical European. And in Paris, people will think you're either mental or stupid if you're just wandering around smiling when there's nothing specific to smile about," I say, flipping through a travel magazine.

"But what if I'm happy?"

I glance up to see if he's joking. He's not. "Then grin, but don't show teeth."

"Seriously, dude?"

"Seriously."

The closer we get to Paris, the jumpier I become, and unable to listen to Faust anymore, I signal the end of the conversation by closing my eyes. And with the lights out, up on my mind's screen pops Kate. I see her face in a film reel of scenes from our shared past: her expression of fear when I grabbed her arm outside Vincent's room the day she found him dormant. Her innocent wonder when I drew her portrait in the café and told her she was beautiful. And the look on her face at the airport when I told her I wasn't coming back to France because I was in love with her. Astonishment. Disappointment. Sadness. All the emotions in a few seconds of reruns.

I skip over the scene where we kissed; I can't even think of that one without the bottom dropping out of me. I focus on when I saw her last: in Paris during the battle against the numa. She hugged me and asked me to stay. Her touch filled me with everything I had been longing for. I had to force myself to break away and run straight back to America so I wouldn't have to see her again. And here I am, halfway across the ocean on my way back to her.

My stomach twists, and I feel sick. I walk over to the minibar and get myself a tonic water. I grab two Perriers, throw one to Faust, and bring the other to Ava. I set it in the slot in her armrest and plop down in the chair closest hers. I don't care if she despises me. I need a distraction.

Ava ignores me as much as you can with someone sitting three feet away from you.

"What are you writing?" I ask.

"Article," she replies.

"On what?" I insist. Since her distaste for me has been established, and I no longer care about making a good impression, there's something deeply gratifying in forcing her to speak to me when she so clearly doesn't want to.

"Art," she says, struggling to keep her eyes on the screen.

"Art. Hmm. Wow, that covers a rather broad range of topics. Are we talking contemporary, old master, medieval? Performance, sculpture, painting, video? Movements, schools, individuals? Art's place in society, politics and art, gender and art . . ."

"Celebrity as commodity in Warhol's portrait series," she says, expecting that to shut me up.

It doesn't. "And you're writing this for . . ."

"*ARTNews* magazine," she says, tapping her finger and glaring at me, as if to ask when the inquisition will be over.

"I assume you're not writing it under your own name?" I prod, genuinely curious now. A lock of wavy hair has fallen down from its pencil perch, and I have the strangest urge to push it back behind her ear. Strange, because I'm sure that if I tried, she would bite my finger off.

She sighs and pushes her laptop an inch away, leaning back in her chair. "I publish under various pseudonyms, each of which is an established, but reclusive, authority in their respective artists. Jemima Hoskins, aka me, just happens to be the leading expert on Warhol in the sixties."

"Doesn't hurt that you were there," I say.

She lets a small smile slip and nods. And as her mask dissolves, I can see her the way her kindred do. She is beautiful. Unique. Magnetic. I can see why Warhol latched onto her, like he did with other offbeat beauties of the day. She pushes the lock of hair behind her ear. Thank God. My impulse disappears and my finger is safe. But her magnetic pull remains.

"You've got an insider's view on the early days of the Factory," I continue. "There aren't too many people around who can claim to have that."

She shakes her head. "Almost everyone's gone."

Now that this door has cracked open, I want to push it further. I want to know this girl. I lean forward, genuinely intrigued. "What were they like? Was it a hotbed of creativity like we had in Paris at the Bateau-Lavoir? Were they as crazy and debauched as the stories say, or was it all a legend to build up the Warhol myth?"

About halfway through my question, Ava's face changes. A memory flickers across her features—I see a flash of vulnerability before she turns back to stone. "Crazy. Debauched. Take your pick," she says, pulling her computer to her and positioning its screen between us like a shield. "Everyone wants to relive the glory days of the Factory. I, for one, am glad they're over."

And that is it. Door shut. End of conversation. End of communication. All the way to Paris.

Chapter Seven

They're waiting for us in the private plane terminal: Ambrose is a huge, hulking form coming at me for a crushing embrace, and Charlotte's a sparkling ball of effervescence, hopping up and down like popcorn and grabbing me around the neck as soon as Ambrose lets go.

"You're here!" she squeals, and then does the jumping thing some more, practically dislocating my neck in the process.

"Couldn't miss the big day," I say, although that's exactly what I had been planning to do. I glance over at Ava, and she's pure cynicism. She knows I'm full of shit. She strides up to Ambrose and holds her hand out.

"Ava Whitefoot," she says.

Ambrose smiles his million-dollar smile and says, "Damn, I miss that accent. Raised in New York?"

"Long Island," Ava responds, and matches his smile watt for watt. And I have to admit: It looks truly genuine. Ava is a people person, except, it seems, when it comes to me.

Charlotte detaches herself from my neck and turns to give Ava the *bises*, leaning up slightly to reach the taller girl's cheeks. "I'm

Charlotte. I don't think we've met."

"I don't go to convocations," Ava explains. "I'm a bit of a hermit. Prefer not to wander far from home."

"Well, we're honored you came all this way for our wedding," Charlotte says, and sticks out her hand for me to inspect the elaborate emerald-and-diamond ring on her left hand.

"Renaissance?" I ask.

"Yes," she says fondly. "Ambrose chose it from the treasury."

"It's exquisite," Ava remarks, looking from the ring to Charlotte's face. "It matches your eyes." She smiles, and the connection is palpable: A new friendship has been born.

Meanwhile, Faust has walked up to Ambrose, and they do a testosterone-charged handshake that makes all their arm muscles bulge. "Faustino Molinaro," Faust says. "Nine eleven."

Ambrose whistles, impressed. "Fire, police, EMT?" he asks.

"New York City Fire Department, Ladder Company Three," Faust replies.

Ambrose clasps Faust by the shoulder and says, "Man, we're honored to have you here. True American hero."

"Not any more than you, from what I've heard," Faust replies. "World War I, first African-American tank battalion. Took out an entire German guard post single-handedly. Man, you're legend among the kindred back home."

Ambrose laughs. "This is home now. And if I get any time off from wedding preparations"—he throws a worried glance at Charlotte, who gives him a happy smile and blows him a kiss— "I'll be happy to show you around."

Ambrose grabs an overstuffed suitcase—Gold has sent gifts for the couple and books for Gaspard. I pick up my own bag and reach for Ava's.

"I've got it," she says crisply, and, taking the bag from me, follows Ambrose and Faust out the door.

Charlotte raises her eyebrows at me and whispers, "Are all New York girls tough like her?"

I put my arm around her, bury my nose in her hair, and breathe in that spring-fresh Charlotte smell. My sister. My kindred. "I don't know about tough," I say, "but they're scary as hell."

~

We pull up to La Maison. The high walls and solid metal entry gates block the view of what lies inside. Then Ambrose buzzes them open, and it's like we're driving into a fairyland. The garden's trees are decorated with tiny glimmering lights, and white and green garlands have been hung atop the massive double front doors.

"Welcome to Wedding Disney," Ambrose jokes, but his expression is one of pure enjoyment. He parks the car next to the fountain, where someone has crowned the angel statue with a flowered head-wreath.

"There's still almost two weeks till the wedding," I say, gesturing at a newly built pagoda with a mountain of chairs stacked inside.

"They got started a month ago. It's mainly Kate and Gaspard going crazy with the decorations, although he pretends he's not as excited as he is," says Ambrose, throwing a love-struck glance toward Charlotte, who is beaming.

I clap him on the back. "Man, I'm really happy for you," I say, and mean it with all my heart. Ambrose and Charlotte found love. Like Vincent and Kate. I never thought I'd say it but they . . . they are the lucky ones.

The doors fly open, and Jeanne bursts through, arms wide, heading straight for me. "*Mon petit Jules*," she cries. "You have come back."

"Just for the wedding," I say, but can't help melting in her maternal arms. Jeanne is the one human presence in La Maison. Her grandmother was the housekeeper when I arrived, and then her mother cared for us as if we were her own. But it is Jeanne who stole my heart. Who acts like a mother hen although I'm a half century older than her.

"You left without saying good-bye," she scolds, and then, when I can't find an easy reply, gives me a look of pity that suggests that she knows exactly why I've stayed away. She's probably known this whole time.

She lowers her voice, although no one is listening. "I had *her* go run some errands. That will give you some time to get settled before you have to see her," she confides.

Yep. She's known this whole time.

"Thank you," I respond, not even trying to deny that I know what she's talking about.

Jeanne nods with satisfaction. She knows that I know that she knows. Which means she can take care of me. Which is exactly what she wants.

Charlotte is leading Ava and Faust into the house, and I follow. Jeanne bustles in behind us, organizing everyone. "Jules, dear, you have your old room, and Ms. Whitefoot and Mr. Molinaro can stay in the east wing," she instructs.

Gaspard appears at the top of the double stairway, wearing an ancient silk waistcoat and a cotton shirt with enormous open cuffs over a pair of high waisted dress pants. "Jeanne, I really don't think period dress is necessary except for the bride and groom," he calls, as he fiddles with a cufflink. And then he looks up and sees us.

His crazy gray-threaded black hair sticks up as if electrified— as per norm—and an uncharacteristic broad smile spreads across his face. "You're here," he says to me, and makes his way down the stairs. "We didn't expect you for another half hour. Traffic must have been light."

"No, but Ambrose was driving," quips Charlotte, provoking a stranglehold bear hug from her fiancé.

"You must be Mademoiselle Whitefoot," says Gaspard, holding a hand out to Ava. But I miss the rest of that introduction, because in from the next room walks Vincent. And his eyes are fixed on me. There's an expression on his face that I can't read, and am not sure I want to. Anger? Disappointment? Betrayal?

Although we spoke briefly on the battlefield, there were other things vying for our attention. Like swinging swords. And flying arrows. I said good-bye when I left. Told him I couldn't stay. But there was blood on our skin and ash on our faces, and I didn't even look him in the eye.

No, the last time we talked—truly communicated—was at the airport in New York. When I told him I was in love with his girlfriend and that it was tearing me apart to see them together. I admitted to my disloyalty. And then abandoned him.

Ignoring the others, he walks straight up to me, eyes burning, and I think for a moment that he's going to hit me. Punch me right in the face. But instead he grabs me and wraps me in his arms, squeezing the breath out of me. And speaking quietly enough that the others can't hear he says, "All's forgotten. There's nothing left to say. I'm just glad you're back. We missed you. All of us."

Chapter Eight

Walking into my room is like traveling back in time. It's like nothing ever happened to drive me away. I breathe in the paper-and-ink smell of my workspace and realize how much I've missed my home. I brush my fingertips over my drafting table and know how much I love my kindred. I belong here, not in New York City. *What the hell is wrong with me?* I think, as I stretch out on my time-worn couch in the middle of my attic room. Surely this thing with Kate isn't traumatic enough to keep me from all of this. My mind wanders and I begin to relax, cocooned in the safety of the familiar surroundings.

And then there is a knock on the door and she walks in. And all those thoughts disappear like smoke in a gust of wind, and the full-on pain hits me square in the chest.

She is ravishing. There is a wild look to her now that she is undead. The look all bardia have, the one that attracts humans, that makes them lay their lives in our hands. It's a complete lack of fear of death. A recklessness coming from knowing we are almost impossible to destroy. And it has turned Kate's natural loveliness into a savage beauty. The golden bardia aura surrounding her amplifies the effect, and my heart has no chance. I am once again lost.

"I'm sorry to barge in on you," she says, and her voice hasn't changed and she is once again the Kate I knew.

I prop up on my elbows and say, "That's okay. Come in," but immediately regret it. I want to see her, but I need her to leave. She sees the struggle in my eyes, and then looks down at the couch—the historic couch, where for a couple of wild, passionate moments she was mine—and her face turns red.

"I didn't try to contact you because I thought you didn't want it," she says.

There's no correct response to that, so I watch her, silent.

"But now that you're here, I was hoping we could talk," she says, still standing in the doorway. She waits, and I have to say something.

"Okay, let's talk." I try to sound nonchalant, but my heart is beating a million miles an hour, and I'm having a hard time breathing. "Let me just open a window." I get up off the damned couch, throw open a couple of windows, and, returning to the rug in the middle of the floor, sit down on it, cross-legged. I motion for her to sit across from me, and she does.

I wait for her to speak, trying to look her in the eyes without flinching. Those eyes. My chest hurts.

"I want to apologize," she begins.

"You don't have to—" I say, but she holds a hand up to stop me.

"I never knew," she says. "I saw how you were with other girls, and I thought I was the same. A harmless flirtation. A bit of fun. I thought you did the things you did and said the things you said just to make me feel good—to get a reaction—not because you meant them."

"That's how it started," I say honestly. She's watching me with sad eyes, and I have to look away. I swing my gaze to the ceiling, run my fingers through my hair, and take a deep breath. Inhale. Exhale. "Then things changed."

"I wouldn't have been as friendly if I had known," she says.

"Then I'm glad you didn't know."

"I wouldn't have allowed Vincent to possess you . . . to use you to kiss me. I wouldn't have let it go that far." There are tears in her eyes.

I don't know what to say. I wish to God that hadn't happened either, because seeing her expression when she realized it wasn't Vincent she was kissing was like a knife to the chest. On the other hand, it was my one and only chance to have her, so I wouldn't have traded it for the world, even with all that pain.

"Come here," I say, and she scoots across the rug toward me until she can lean into my open arms. I hold her while she cries and feel something inside me snap into place. A piece of me that began shifting when I walked through the front door and realized this is where I belong. I am finally accepting it. This is the only way it will ever be between me and Kate. And it hurts like hell, but there's nothing to do about it except to pick myself up and move on.

"I'm the one who should apologize," I tell her. "I wasn't honest. But really, how could I be?" We lean back, and she wipes her eyes and nods.

"I know," she says. "I've thought about it. You couldn't tell me without betraying Vincent. You couldn't tell Vincent because . . . what would be the point? I understand why you left. It was really the only sane, healthy thing you could do. But you need to know how much I miss you. That you are one of my favorite people, my closest friends. I wish you could come back, but also realize it's totally selfish of me. So I just want to know that you are fine. That you are happy where you are."

"I'm fine and I'm happy," I lie.

Kate searches my eyes. "No, you're not."

"I will be," I say. "Promise. More time, and I'll be fine."

She takes a deep breath and hugs her legs to her chest. Like old Kate. A moment passes before she speaks again. "It was good of you to come to the wedding."

"I didn't want to," I admit.

"I know," she says, and smiles sadly. "So who are these New York kindred Theodore sent with you?"

"Well, Faust is a newbie, and one of the nicest guys I ever met," I respond. "And Ava scares the crap out of me and, for some reason that completely eludes me, hates my guts. But Gold wanted me to accompany her here so she could quiz Gaspard and Bran, and I'm sure you and Vincent as well, about what to do about the numa in New York."

"Is Ava Gold's second?" Kate asks curiously.

"They don't have firsts and seconds there. Or at least, not on paper, although it's pretty clear to me that Gold's in charge. She's his special envoy, in any case."

Kate looks thoughtful. "Why does she hate you? Did you hit on her?"

"Absolute negative on that. It was apparently loathing at first sight," I say.

Kate grabs my hands, and we lean back, using each other's weight to stand up, both cracking a smile at the effort it takes to get off the ground.

"Dinner?" she asks.

"A meal in the presence of France's brave Champion?" I say. "How can I resist?"

Kate smiles and puts her arm around me, resting her head on my shoulder as we walk together toward the door.

Chapter Nine

Dinner in the kitchen—it's just like old times. Jeanne bustles between the stove and table, bringing course after delicious course, and Ambrose inhales everything like an industrial-size vacuum cleaner. Charlotte sits next to him, so close that her body is practically fused to his, chatting away in English to Ava, who has proven once again to be the star of the show. In less than an hour, she's got everyone at La Maison wrapped around her finger.

Gaspard and Jean-Baptiste always took their meals upstairs, but now that his partner is gone, Gaspard seems to have decided to join the rest of the group. He looks distinctly awkward, struggling to understand Faust's strong New York accent as he quizzes the young bardia about New York's kindred. There is a sadness about Gaspard that is hard to watch. He's lost weight, and his hyper quirkiness has mellowed with his grief. But since he is here, eating with the rest of the house, it means he is trying. He's making an effort to carry on. I can't imagine losing someone you've loved for over a century and a half. Up until recently, I couldn't even imagine loving someone at all.

At Gaspard's side, Kate is radiant inside this warm circle of conversation and companionship. She belongs here—it is evident. My eyes sweep the table and meet Ava's. She glances back and forth between me and Kate, and I can see her catching on, and suddenly I'm choking on the chicken I was trying to swallow. Ava gets this amused look and turns back to her conversation with Charlotte.

Ambrose pats me on the back. "You got to chew, dude."

"You're one to talk—human shovel," I reply, taking a quick sip of water.

"Need the calories. Wedding prep is taking more out of me than fighting numa ever did," he says. Charlotte nudges him, and then gives him a kiss on the cheek. Kate sees it and takes Vincent's hand under the table. Love is freaking everywhere. I clear my throat.

"So, Gaspard, when is Bran coming?" I ask in English, so that our guests can follow along. "Gold specifically wanted Ava to meet with him."

"Ah, you see, there's a bit of a problem with that," Gaspard replies. "The mother of Bran's sons is indisposed. I believe she is in the hospital—nothing too serious, fortunately. But Bran must care for his children and won't be coming to the wedding."

"Then we have to go to him!" Ava blurts out.

Gaspard places his hand on hers. "That is the plan, my dear. Bran has invited you to visit him in Brittany this weekend."

"How do I get there?" she asks. This change in plans seems to set her on edge: She's squeezing her fork so tightly that her knuckles are white.

"The easiest way is by car. I would be happy to accompany you, but with all the wedding preparations, I'm afraid—"

"I'll take her," I say, cutting Gaspard off. Ava stares at me in surprise. "Gold wanted me to be your French tour guide," I explain, even though that's not really the reason. I'm not really sure why I'm offering—it has something to do with her panic and the feeling that I need to do something to help.

"Yes, of course, that would be best," Gaspard says.

"Faust can be our third," Ava adds quickly.

"No can do," Faust says. "I'll be sleeping the sleep of the dead."

"You're dormant this weekend?" Ava asks, accusation in her tone.

"Hey, I was awake to accompany you on the plane," Faust says with a shrug, "and I'll be awake again for the wedding and the trip home. You can find another third for the trip to Brittany, right?"

"Don't worry about your safety getting there and back," Vincent reassures Ava. "Numa activity is at a record low in France—you won't need a third."

"Thanks to Kate's super-Champion-numa vision," interjects Ambrose.

Kate responds by blowing cockily on her fingernails, and then grins as Ambrose laughs.

"How far is Bran's house?" Ava asks, looking distinctly uneasy.

"Paris to Carnac is about five hundred kilometers," Gaspard responds. Ava gives him a blank stare.

"Americans don't think in kilometers," Ambrose explains. "That's a four-and-a-half-hour drive."

Ava gives me a pained look, and I'm sure my face is a mirror image. A six-hour plane trip was bad enough with Faust serving as a buffer. Now we have to drive four and a half hours in a car. Alone.

Chapter Ten

The next four days are a blur of activity. Once it's decided that Ava and I will leave for Brittany on Saturday, she practically disappears. Kate and Charlotte enlist her help with the wedding preparations and, on their breaks, take her to see the sights of Paris. On one of the rare occasions that our paths cross, I ask how her research for Gold is going.

"I have to start with Bran," she claims, and that's the end of that.

I spend the time catching up with my kindred over meals, sparring in the armory, and walking the Paris streets. In a way, it's like nothing ever happened, but my return to New York lurks, ever-present, in the back of my mind.

Vincent and I spend the next few evenings in the great hall, sprawled on the leather couches, catching up. People come and go, knowing we will be there, and join the conversation, before leaving us alone once again.

Vincent wants to know about New York, and I give him all the details. But we both carefully skirt around the subject of Kate and her everyday life with my kindred. It's unnatural to feel this uncomfortable around my best friend. We know everything there is to know about each other. But we're both being careful. Tiptoeing around each other's feelings. And knowing that we both feel weird about it.

Although we don't sleep, everyone needs their downtime, and in the early hours of Saturday morning, I say good night to Vincent and go back to my room. I try to read but can't focus. I pull some old drawings out of a cupboard and sort through them. God, I'm glad no one dug through my stuff while I was gone. All the drawings from the months before I left are of Kate. Kate lying on a couch, reading. Kate sitting in a café, laughing. Kate in my studio, lying on her back and staring dreamily at the ceiling as she poses for me.

I toss the sheaf of papers onto a table and realize I'm no longer pining. Following the conversation with Kate, I've begun to pull myself back together and am starting to feel like my old self again. Maybe, when I get back from Brittany, I'll talk Ambrose into going to one of the clubs we used to go to. I could pick up a high-spirited French beauty. Charm her into taking me back to her place. And find solace in the arms of a woman for a few delicious hours. I think back to the last time . . . it's been awhile. Sacha? Or was it Sandra? I can't even remember her name.

And suddenly I feel empty. Like a century of affairs that felt like a bubbling source of sparkling springwater—water I needed to survive—had actually just been a mirage. A dry streambed in a desert of emotional void. And I know that's not what I want anymore. I crave something else. Something real, tangible, lasting.

I pick out a sketchpad and some charcoal and take them over to my easel. Who to draw . . . that's not Kate. I start sketching the lines of Faust's face. Handsome, square jawline. Deep-set eyes and defined brows. I smile when I think of his unself-conscious earnestness. His natural openness. And I add a few shadows to his cheekbones and some white to his forehead, and here he comes, emerging from the paper. Faustino Molinaro: a hero with a heart.

Satisfied, I flip the paper over the back of the easel and start from scratch. I draw without thinking, my hand moving while my mind drifts back across the ocean to that foreign place I've made my home. New York: where I speak the language but don't yet understand the people. It is still a beautiful mystery to me—the danger that lurks just beyond people's everyday lives, the vertiginous mix of nationalities, ethnicities, languages, foods, dress, religions . . . everything in the world condensed into one shining city.

I am drawing New York, it's New York in my mind, but staring out at me from the surface of the paper are the eyes of Ava. Exotic eyes, whose color I haven't yet figured out. *For fear of getting freezer burn.* High cheekbones. I pick up a copper-brown pastel and brush it across her face. Warm-dark skin that seems to glow from within. Bow lips, the color of currants.

I sit back and inspect my work. New York. Ava. They are the same in my mind. The same on the page. I can see what people love, what draws her kindred. . . and apparently mine as well—to her. There's something about her that makes you want to get closer. To be near her. To have her accept you into her court of admirers. *Well, that's not going to happen for you, buddy,* I think. *You're going to have to make your own friends.* A few days in Paris haven't made her warm to me, it seems. She ignores me at the rare meals we've all had together and was as glacial as ever when we crossed paths in the garden this morning.

There's a knock on my door. I yell, *"Entrez!"* and it cracks open. And, holy crap, speak of the devil. I flip the page with Faust back over, covering Ava's portrait before she's able to get a glance.

She steps into the room. "Sorry for disturbing you," she says, and then, getting a glimpse of my jam-packed walls, begins the gawking process that everyone who walks into my room goes through.

"Wow!" she says, starting at one wall and working her way up and down the rows of portraits. "Are these your saves?"

"Yeah, well, I've had a hundred years of rescues," I say. "Demands a lot of wall space." I stay seated on my stool, body-blocking the sketchpad where her portrait hides under Faust's.

"I'd say!" she says, stopping at a portrait of a little girl I saved from drowning in the 1960s. "She's a beauty," she remarks.

"Went on to found an NGO in Africa. Her group has saved countless lives," I say. "One of those times where your sacrifice pays off big for humanity."

Ava moves on to another—a rough kid with glazed-over eyes and a hollow face. "Unlike others," I continue, "who, even after you've saved them, manage to finish themselves off anyway." She gives me a quick look of understanding and moves on, perusing my walls like a gallery.

"You *are* talented," she says.

"Why, thank you," I respond, half-curious. "But weren't you the one who introduced me to your clan as an accomplished artist?"

"Honestly," Ava says, "I'd never seen anything of yours in person. Just some black-and-white photos from old exhibition catalogues . . . before your death, of course. I have no idea what pseudonyms you've been using since then."

"There have been several," I admit.

"Yeah, well, let's just say your reputation preceded you," she says, and gives me a significant look. But what it signifies, I have absolutely no clue.

She strolls over to the couch and, before I can stop her, picks up the sheaf of drawings I tossed there.

"No, wait!" I say, jumping up and lunging toward the stack,

but it's too late, she's already shuffling through. Kate after Kate after Kate. She stops at one: a drawing of Kate looking up from her *café crème*. Her eyes are sparkling, and she has a playful smile on her lips. Vincent asked me to draw it from a photo he took of her. I didn't tell him that I made a copy for myself.

Ava stares at the drawing and then up at me. She's put the pieces together. Smart girl. Damned insightful. "She's why you ran away."

I tuck the pages back into the cabinet and then sit back down on my stool. "I didn't exactly run away."

She lifts an eyebrow.

"Okay, I ran away," I admit.

"I've seen how you are with your kindred," she says. "How close you are. You're practically family." She pauses, and then asks, "Vincent loved her first, right?"

I nod and rub my forehead with my fingertips.

"It was the noble thing to do," she says quietly. She strolls over to me and inspects the image of Faust. Her own portrait is faintly visible through the paper, and I'm supremely glad in this moment that X-ray vision is not a revenant superpower. She smiles fondly. "Good old Faust. You really captured his spirit here. I don't think I know a nicer guy in all of New York."

"Yeah, well, that good old guy's lying dormant in the east wing right now," I say. "Useless as our third man for Brittany."

"That's what I wanted to talk about. When do you think we can leave?" she asks, and chews anxiously on a fingernail. Ava's nervous. She sees me notice and drops her hand and squares her shoulders, slipping back into her armor.

"We can leave at daybreak if you want," I suggest. "That way you get to see some of the French countryside. I'm not a half-bad tour guide, I suppose. I've been pretty much everywhere."

She shakes her head and says, "Now."

My eyes widen. "Excuse me?"

"Sorry," she says, and her leg is jiggling. "I'm just feeling impatient. I have so much to talk to Bran about, and it would be nice to get going. Like, really soon. Now, if possible."

I shrug. "Now works for me. Let me just grab some clothes, and I'll meet you down in the kitchen. We can pack some stuff from the fridge so we don't have to eat fast food on the autoroute."

"I'll take care of that," she says, and in a flash she's halfway out my door. "Meet you in ten?"

Americans—always in a rush, I think, while saying, "Ten it is."

She closes the door, and I breathe a sigh of relief. I lift up the sketch of Faust to look at my drawing of her, comparing it to the woman who was just standing inches away from me. It is spot on. And there's something about it. Something a little too true. Sometimes the muse does that when you create ... drawing, painting, writing ... she gives you insight into the soul of a near stranger or a clear picture of a situation you couldn't have known existed. And then when you find out it is true, you know you've been used. You're just a tool of the muse.

The muse gave me a view into Ava. And something inside me is glad she didn't see it. With one last look at my portrait of New York, I leave my easel and begin packing my bag.

Chapter Eleven

We drive for the first hour in silence, Ava flipping through the radio stations until we get too far from Paris to get anything but static and then changing to the iPod Ambrose gave us. His playlists are full of jazz: Louis Armstrong and Ella Fitzgerald scat and sing and croon while we drive with the windows down. Ava's head is tilted back, eyes closed, as she breathes in the fresh morning air of the countryside.

But after a while, the noncommunication gets old, and I feel like talking. Ava hasn't said a word since we left. Finally I turn the music down. "So where are you from?" I ask.

"Are you making conversation?" Ava responds, amusement twinkling in her eyes.

"Yes, I suppose I am," I reply. "In fact, I'm the driver and you're the drivee, which means you're responsible for keeping me entertained."

"There's the music," she says.

"An hour of jazz is quite enough for me, thank you. So, back to the question. Where are you from?"

She was hoping to brush me off, and my insistence bothers

her. She raises her eyebrows defiantly. "I don't see why I have to tell you my life story."

"And I don't see why you've been acting like I'm your own personal public enemy number one since the moment you laid eyes on me." Wow. I didn't mean to say that.

Ava squeezes her eyes shut and pinches the top of her nose. She breathes in and out, and then says, "I'm from Long Island."

"I mean your family," I prod. "Where are they from?"

She stares at me. "You mean you want to know what race I am?"

Now I'm afraid. I know about this political correctness thing in the States, and never know which terms are currently acceptable and which will get you slapped. What I wanted to know was the origin of the glowing copper skin, the thick, black, flowing hair that frames her face, the almond-shaped eyes that are . . . I pull my gaze from the road to her face for a second. . . an extraordinary tone between brown and dark green. I wanted to know what factors merged to give her such an original beauty. But something tells me not to compliment her, so I play it safe. "Well, that wasn't exactly the way I was thinking about it, but sure . . . race . . . , " I respond carefully. "Why not?"

She gapes at me for a count, and then bursts out laughing. "Okay, then. One grandma is African American, one grandpa Cherokee."

"He must be the Whitefoot," I say, and she nods.

"And my mom's side is Dutch, Scottish, Irish, I think there's even a French Huguenot in there. I *am* the American melting pot," she says, with not a little bit of pride.

"You're New York," I murmur.

"What?" she asks.

"Nothing."

We ride in silence for a moment while I savor the information she's given me. It's been a long time since I've had a one-on-one conversation with a woman that didn't consist of logistics in rescuing a human, and I've forgotten how the give-and-take feeds me. Every tidbit she offers is like honey . . . a piece of herself. Especially from this woman who gives nothing away. At least to me. Which reminds me . . .

"So why do you hate me?" I ask.

Her lightheartedness disappears, only to be replaced by the habitual coldness. Not quite as glacial as before, I note. But it would still qualify as refrigerated.

"I don't hate you," she says, sighing. "I just hate your type."

"My type," I huff. "And just what would that be?"

"A rake. A scoundrel," she responds.

"Now just a moment," I say, hitting the button on my door to roll up the windows. I need to hear this. "What are you talking about?"

"As I've said before, your reputation precedes you," Ava says, and now all warmth is gone. Her arms are crossed, and she is as closed as a safe.

I think back to the council meeting, where I saw her first. "Is this about what Harlem Riots guy said about me seducing half of London at the last convocation?"

"That was just one of the plethora of stories I had already heard."

"Plethora? You heard a *plethora* of stories about me?" I ask, voice raised.

"Showgirls, politicians, even a princess, from what I heard," she says crisply. "No one is immune to the wiles of Jules Marchenoir."

I pull the car to the side of the road, put it in park, and unstrap my seat belt so that I can face her. "Okay. For one thing, you Americans must have way too much time on your hands, or way too little happening in your own country, if all you have to discuss is the love lives of your foreign kindred."

She shrugs. "The French have always fascinated us, I admit. Especially those who live up to all the worst stereotypes."

"All the worst—" I exclaim. "Just what the—" I feel like I'm choking, I'm so angry.

"Water?" Ava says coolly, and hands me a bottle of Evian from the bag she packed.

I take it, twist off the top, guzzle half of it, and then pour some in my hand and splash it on my face. I don't care if I get Ambrose's leather upholstery wet. I need to cool down.

"Better?" Ava asks with a grin.

"Stop it with the smugness," I say, and she gives me a look like she just won the grand prize by getting under my skin.

I take a deep breath and say, "Okay, first of all, I am not a rake. I have never treated a woman disrespectfully. I have never lied, cheated, or misled a woman about my intentions or commitment. Yes, I have seen a lot of women in my life, but I have treated them all impeccably, made them each feel like royalty—including the princess—and made sure that each of them . . . every one . . . thought that it was *her* choice not to see me again."

"I have a very hard time believing that," Ava says, eyes narrowed.

"Ask my kindred. Hell, ask the ladies in question . . . those who are still alive. I have no doubt in my mind that each and every one of them would remember me with fondness. Maybe even with pity at 'breaking my heart.'"

Ava is silent.

"Besides, why the hell do you care?" I say with raised voice. "Are you some kind of feminist crusader who has to protect your poor hapless sisters from the evil wiles of men? Trust me, Ava, the women I've known have not been weak. I have preyed on no one.

They've all been as strong as me, if not stronger."

There's a look on her face that I can't interpret—a look of hurt and pride and defensiveness all at once. And then, suddenly, I understand.

"Something bad happened to you."

"Yes," she responds.

"It had something to do with the Factory," I say, remembering her reaction on the plane.

"Yes." She pauses, deciding whether she's going to tell me, and then says, "If I've judged you unfairly—"

"Oh, believe me, you have," I interject.

"Which I haven't yet made my mind up about," she continues, "I owe you an explanation for my—"

"Vehemence," I suggest.

She looks surprised, and then accepts it. "Okay . . . vehemence." She sighs. "So . . . the Factory. I was a student, studying art history at NYU. I wasn't an artist myself, but all my friends were artists, writers, musicians. It was New York in the sixties, and the city was practically exploding with creativity and a crazy kind of try-anything quest for expression."

I nod. That was like the Paris of my human days . . . I know exactly what she's talking about.

"The first time I was brought to Andy's, he latched onto me. Called me his muse. His 'It Girl.' He filmed me. Painted me. Wanted me around all the time. Introduced me to everyone who was anyone, and they made me the toast of the town. I lapped it up, the instant celebrity. But Andy had other favorites, of course, and one of those was an artist named Rosco."

The moment she says his name, I know who she's talking about. And I can predict how the story's going to go. Badly. At best.

"He was incredibly handsome and so charismatic. Everyone

wanted to be around him all the time. So he and I were"—she presses the tips of her index fingers together—"the It couple. We were at all the parties. He was the king of the downtown gallery scene, and I was his queen. He was crazy about me, and I was madly in love with him. After a year, he asked me to marry him. I said yes."

She pauses and takes a sip of her water. "On the surface things seemed too good to be true. But underneath, things were already spiraling out of control, only we were living at such a frenzied pace, I didn't even realize it. You've heard of Andy's parties, right?" she asks.

"Sex, drugs, and rock 'n' roll," I answer honestly. No two ways about it. The Factory was all about debauchery.

She nods, and I sense a weight of regret. "Were you into it too?" I ask.

"I wasn't into the worst of it. But . . ." She studies her hands for a moment before looking back at me. "Not all of us were angels before we grew our wings."

She's right about that. You don't become a bardia from living a pure human life. You become it by sacrificing yourself to save someone. Which is, I assume, the part she's about to get to.

"We had this party at a big old abandoned theater in the Bronx. The place was dilapidated. The party had been going all night, and everyone was pretty out of it. There were too many people standing on this one balcony, pretty high up. It was like this theater box that would seat ten, but there were thirty people crowded on it. I was on the ground floor, waving up to Rosco, when I saw the supports start to crumble. Pieces of plaster were coming off and falling to the ground. I screamed at him to get everybody off, but he couldn't hear me, and no one else would pay attention. Like I said, everyone was wasted."

Ava looks out the window, remembering. "I book it up three

flights of stairs and try to tell people what's happening, but they won't listen. I start pulling them off, and they're all yelling at me, including Rosco. And then the balcony's floor cracks and everyone makes a rush for the door, and suddenly it's just me and this one girl who's so strung out she can barely stand, in a crumbling theater box leaning out over the floor thirty feet below. Rosco's standing one foot on, one foot off, holding his hand out to help us, and I'm trying to pass the girl to him, but she's so high she doesn't know what's going on. The moment he grabs her, the floor gives out, and I fall to my death. Broken neck, plus crushed by falling masonry. I got the double whammy."

"I'm sorry," I whisper, because there isn't anything else to say.

"Theodore saw my light," she says. "Corpse-napped me from the mortuary before they could cremate me. Funeral director didn't want to get in trouble, so he didn't tell anyone my body was missing and gave my parents someone else's ashes.

"The first time I was volant—just weeks after I died—I went to find Rosco. And I found a lot more than I had bargained for. He was with the stoned girl from the party. He had been with her for a long time; they were engaged. And there were others. Lots of others."

"He wasn't a rake," I say, "he was a psychopath." I want to reach for her, to touch her hand . . . offer her some comfort, but I can tell she doesn't want that.

"Yeah, well. I was afraid I was going to have to stay away from Manhattan for longer—so he wouldn't see me. But he died a few years later from an overdose, and most of the others I knew either did the same or scattered by the eighties. By then, I was used to my little haven in Brooklyn and was happy to have a river between me and anything to do with the limelight."

"But you haven't really left it behind. You still write about it," I say. "The expert on Warhol and his crowd."

She shrugs, but I can tell I hit a sore spot. "It's a type of redemption, I suppose," she concedes, her voice breaking slightly. Her eyes are glassy, but she's not letting herself cry. "I guess I'm still trying to figure it all out."

Seeing that she's done talking, I start the car and pull back out onto the highway. "I understand the vehemence now," I say after a moment.

She gives a little laugh. "Yeah. I'm sorry about that. I misjudged you."

I nod. "Apology accepted. Does this mean that I am now free from the stink-eye?"

"If you promise never to call me Frosty again," she says with a smile.

I gasp. "When did I—"

Ava cuts me off. "During our standoff with the numa. Ryan heard you muttering it under your breath."

"The traitor!" I say. "He's never walking volant with me again." I glance over at her, and she's laughing. Not crying. This is a good thing.

"No stink-eye, no Frosty," I promise.

"Deal," she agrees, and reaches over to turn up the music.

Chapter Twelve

When we arrive at Bran's, a revenant boy meets us at the gate. Although I never met Louis—he was dead, killed by Violette, by the time I arrived at the battle—it can't be anyone else. The turncoat numa's bloodred aura has mellowed into a deep golden color, a visual effect I've never seen before.

Vincent told me all about him last night: how, when he animated after sacrificing himself for Kate, his aura had already begun to change. Bran took him under his wing and whisked him far away from the city, and any numa who might target him as a traitor, until Louis's transition to bardia could be complete. Whatever he's doing seems to be working. The bitter, hopeless kid Vincent described is nowhere to be seen in the smiling boy unlatching the gate for us.

We steer into a courtyard lined with apple trees and rosebushes. The ancient stone house at the end of the drive is entirely covered in purple-flowered wisteria vines.

"*Bienvenue*," Louis says as we step out of the car. He gives me the *bises*, and then walks around to Ava. "Welcome, I am called Louis," he says, and shakes her hand. "This is all I know to say in

English," he admits, with a comically strong accent.

"*Et vous le parlez parfaitement*," she replies in impeccable French, and gives him one of her blinding smiles. The kid doesn't stand a chance: One look and he's under her spell.

I stand there speechless for all of a second, and then say, "Wait a minute, Ava. You speak French?"

She smiles. *"Oui."*

"Well, why didn't you tell me?"

"You didn't ask," she says simply. She lets Louis pick up her bag, and when he holds out his arm, she laces hers through it and walks with him toward the house.

After hours in the car, I need to stretch my legs, and, instead of following them inside, take a path around the house to what I think must be the backyard.

And what I see when I emerge from the curtain of trailing wisteria vines stops me in my tracks. Bran's house was built on the edge of a field of standing stones. The stones of Carnac: five-thousand-year-old megalithic menhirs lined up in rows and columns, like a prehistoric graveyard. France's version of Stonehenge is in Bran's backyard.

I don't know why I'm surprised. He comes from a line of mystical *guérisseurs* that stretches back many generations. What better place for a magical healer to grow up than on a place thought—by those who believe in such things—to be one of earth's energy centers?

Through the morning mist, I spot a lone figure trudging between the menhirs toward me. He raises an arm in welcome, and I walk down into the stones to meet him. There's no mistaking Bran: wild black hair, scarecrow figure, and bottle-thick glasses magnifying his owlish eyes. Although his appearance hasn't changed in the last few months, there is an easiness to his stride that he didn't have in Paris. Brittany is obviously his land.

He belongs here.

We reach each other, and he leans in to give me the four *bises* traditional in the countryside. "Just dropped my boys off at a friend's house," he says, gesturing toward the town on the far end of the field of stones. "That'll give us some time to talk alone." We head back toward the house.

"How are you faring in New York?" he asks, inspecting my face as if he can read the answer there.

"Fine," I say, thrusting my hands into my pockets as I step over the pieces of a crumbled stone. "I didn't plan to come back so soon, but I'm on a special mission from Gold."

He nods. "Theodore actually invited me to return to New York. Claimed I had a lot to teach them, especially now that some new issues have arisen, or so he said. But I told him that once in a lifetime is my limit for transatlantic trips. Not that I didn't enjoy it. I just don't like to be that far from home."

"Yes, well, he sent his emissary instead," I say. "I'm sure she'll have a lot to ask you. I was planning on translating, but just discovered she speaks perfect French. So it seems I'm only serving as chauffeur."

"Whatever the reason, I'm more than happy to welcome you to my home. You were the first revenant I ever laid eyes on. That day marked the beginning of my life's true path."

We walk up a narrow set of steps and into Bran's grassy back garden to see Louis carrying a tray of food out the back door. He places it on a round white garden table that's been set for lunch. "You're back," he says, "just in time for sandwiches."

Ava steps out with a pitcher of water. "Where do you want me to put this?" she asks Louis in French. She turns and, seeing us, yells, "Oh, hello!"

Bran looks up, and when his eyes meet hers, it's like everything stops. And then restarts in slow motion.

Bran ducks his head and raises a hand in front of his face, like he's shielding his eyes from a blinding light. "An aura that blazes like a star on fire," he murmurs.

Ava gets this look on her face like she's just gotten word that someone died. The pitcher in her hand starts shaking, splashing water on the grass. She slowly leans over and sets it on the table, and then stands again to face Bran.

She's in shock, but she's not confused, like I am for a few seconds before the realization dawns on me.

Ava suspected. Gold suspected. That's why she's here, to consult Bran not as *guérisseur*, but as VictorSeer.

"Jules," he says, turning his head to squint at me from behind his raised hand. "You've brought me another Champion."

Chapter Thirteen

Ava didn't cry in the car when she told me about her death. Or even when she described her fiancé's betrayal. But she's crying now. She stands there hugging herself, tears rolling down her cheeks and chin raised, like she's ready to face her doom.

I make a move toward her, but Bran gets there first, squinting so hard his eyes are practically closed. He puts his arms around her, and she lets him lead her into the house. "Louis, bring Ava some water," he calls, and Louis scrambles for the pitcher. I follow them into an old-fashioned parlor set with overstuffed chairs and jam-packed with odd objects. Bran deposits Ava onto a couch that has so many pillows there's barely room to sit. He yanks an ancient crocheted blanket off the back of it and wraps it around her shoulders.

Her face is in her hands now. I look frantically around the room, spot a box of tissues between a golden hand reliquary and a stuffed fox, and leap for it. "Thank you," Bran says, taking it from me as he wedges himself between the pillows next to the weeping girl. "If you could perhaps give us a bit of time . . . ," he suggests.

"Are you sure?" I ask, feeling suddenly responsible for leaving Ava with people she's barely met.

"Go ahead. I'll be fine," says Ava from behind her fingers. So I go.

Louis's making his way into the house with the glass of water, his face etched with concern. He obviously has no clue what's going on but looks eager to help. I'm the only one here without a role.

I brush out past him and look at the lunch spread on the table, but feel too weird to sit there by myself with Ava having a breakdown just yards away. So I grab a sandwich and set off among the menhirs.

I end up walking to the beach, a mile away, and sit on a boulder watching the waves as I eat. Now that the initial shock of discovering that Ava is a Champion has worn off, I'm trying to understand why this news is so traumatic for her. I run back over the story she told me in the car and realize she's spent the last fifty years keeping people at arm's length. Living a convenient distance from the Warehouse, but not in it. Mingling with her kindred when she felt like it—obviously enjoying the contact when she was there—but able to go home to a life by herself. She's been trying for a quiet existence—the opposite of what she had at the Factory. No drama. No limelight. No one to count on who could let her down. Self-sufficient.

Now all that would change. She would once again become the center of attention. The entirety of New York's bardia—and probably kindred farther away—will be looking to her to lead them. This has got to be the very last thing she would want.

I finish my sandwich and walk for miles along the coastline, killing time. Thinking. A few hours pass before I make my way back, taking a different path in order to pass the famous gargantuan menhir locals call "the Giant." I finally find it, not far from Bran's, standing on its own in the middle of a field. And there, at its base, is Ava, legs bent up against her chest, chin on her knees, lost in thought.

I walk over to her, the setting sun casting my elongated shadow at her feet, and she lifts her head. She's composed now, the tears long gone.

"May I?" I ask, gesturing to the ground in front of her.

"Be my guest," she says.

I lower myself to sit cross-legged facing her. My legs almost touch her feet, but I am careful not to get too close. She gives me a sad grin.

"Not the news you were hoping for?" I ask.

She shakes her head. "But not a complete surprise. Things have been happening for a while. My vision changing. My perceptions altering. I didn't know what it was at first, so I didn't tell anyone about it. But then, when the New York revenants you took to the battle in Paris returned with stories about Kate and her powers, I went to talk to Gold.

"He informed me of the Champion's 'qualifications' as per Gaspard: anterior powers of persuasion, perception, and communication, and the rest. It all seemed so vague—like it could apply to anyone."

I shake my head. "Not anyone. Especially persuasion. That one's a no-brainer. From what you told me about the Factory days, everyone was drawn to you—practically enchanted by you. And seeing how you interact with your New York kindred, I'd say that hasn't changed."

I pause. Breathe. "You're a lot like Kate in that way. She charmed everyone at La Maison. She even got Jean-Baptiste to let her into the house before he knew who she was. But it wasn't a surface-level thing. She wasn't using her charms to manipulate us. We were charmed because she was honestly good. A genuine person who cared about others and wasn't in it for herself. Which seems a lot like you."

Ava squeezes her eyes together, and then exhales hard. She holds out a hand to me, and I take it and scoot forward until her feet are tucked under my legs. And then I wait.

Finally she speaks. "Bran says there's no question. I've just come into my powers. For the last couple of weeks, I've been seeing these crazy red columns of light at a distance. I thought something was wrong with my eyes. Or my mind. Something that would fix itself the next time I was dormant. But when I awoke, it was still there. Bran says Kate has the same thing—it shows her where numa are located."

She looks at me for confirmation. I nod.

She winces, then continues. "And for the last few weeks, I've been able to hear my kindred's thoughts if they're directed toward me. When I tried, I was able to speak to Theodore's mind. That's when he decided to send me here."

"Try now," I say. "Tell me something."

Ava looks me in the eyes, and in the same way I hear a volant spirit speak to my mind, I hear her say, *I don't want to be the Champion, Jules.*

Yep. She's got the Champion mind-speak. "Why?" I respond aloud. "Because you're going to be the focus of attention again? Because if it's just a matter of self-doubt, I've got to tell you, Ava— you are capable. Fate, or whatever, wouldn't have chosen you if you weren't."

Ava bites her lip. "Even if I'm capable . . . I don't want it. I wish it were anyone else. What am I going to do, Jules?"

I reach forward and take her hands in mine. "I'll tell you what you're going to do, Ava. You're going to be the strongest leader New York's kindred have ever seen. You've got it in you. That's as clear as day. The way people watched you at the council meeting, crowded around you afterward, listened to every word you said—you're a natural-born leader. And the day we walked together, you handled that situation better than any seasoned bardia I've seen: You commanded your team with precision, were merciless with your foes, and not only managed the humans on the spot, but from what I heard, made sure they got protection from their numa contacts afterward."

She smiles at me sadly.

"Ava, you have not only survived the dark side of human selfishness without it crushing you, but you adapted to your immortality by building a safe life for yourself where you could handle the fallout from your human years. I have no question you'll find a way to carve out a niche for the privacy that you need within the public role you're going to have to accept. And do you know why?" I ask.

"Why?" she responds.

"Because, Ava, you are supremely kick-ass."

She bursts out laughing.

"And don't think I give that compliment to just anyone," I continue with a playful grin. "No, that one's got to be earned. You started by scaring the crap out of me, and now that I know you better and am a little less frightened, you impress me to no end."

She shakes her head, and her smile is irrepressible. And I feel like I've just won the lottery for bringing that out in her. For making her happy. It's kind of like the expansive, helium-balloon feeling I used to have when I flirted with a girl—flattered her ego with beautiful words. But back then, I was doing it for myself too. To get something in return: a kiss, a date, a night.

This time it's one-way only. I know she doesn't like me, I mean ... at least she doesn't still hate me. But it is exceedingly clear that making Ava feel good will get me nowhere. And that is actually fine.

I am sitting in a Brittany field, next to a prehistoric monument, in the presence of a woman who embodies New York for me, when I have my revelation. I realize I am ready to put aside my sadness in order to follow the possibility of doing something good.

I've been focusing this whole time on what I wanted—what I thought I needed—and suffering because I couldn't have it. Maybe my road to recovery will involve turning that on its head and focusing on giving someone else what *they* need.

Ava needs a friend right now. Someone to lean on. Someone to help her with the challenge she faces. I could be that person for her. And with this flash of inspiration, I finally feel I've turned a page.

Chapter Fourteen

We return to Paris the next day. Ava is too deep in thought to want conversation. I respect her silence and fill the hours with old French songs that I find on Ambrose's iPod, singing along heartily to Edith Piaf and Michel Polnareff, which makes her smile. And my resolve to pour my energy into supporting Ava suddenly seems like the most brilliant idea I've ever had. A smiling Ava is definitely something I could get used to.

Bran makes sure the news of a new Champion precedes us to La Maison, and the welcome when we arrive is enthusiastic to the point of overwhelming Ava once again. She stays in her room for the first day, after taking some books from Gaspard's library, claiming she needs to catch up on Champion lore. But after hiding out for twenty-four hours, she suddenly appears, ready to meet with my kindred to mine them for information and talk strategy.

And though the wedding preparations seem to multiply and accelerate, and the house begins filling with guests, everyone makes it a priority to spend time with Ava. She gratefully accepts my self-appointed role of assistant and counselor and rewards me with a smile every time she sees me waiting for her in the corner of the library that Gaspard designated for the informal meetings.

While Kate talks with Ava about the particulars of her experience as Champion, I take mental notes as to how I, and the New York revenants, can make things easier for her. How some of the weight of her responsibility can be placed on others. How an infrastructure can be set up to support her.

When Vincent and Gaspard talk about their strategy in ridding France of the numa and their influence, I act as Ava's counsel, helping her formulate how the French approach can be modified to work in the New World. Although I've been steeped in French tradition, I'm beginning to have a feeling for how things work in New York, and Ava welcomes my ideas with enthusiasm. She begins to look at me with new eyes, grateful for my help. I am earning her respect and am surprised by how gratifying that is to me.

~

Meanwhile, love has struck once again in La Maison. Charles and his German clan arrive first thing Tuesday morning, just as Faust awakes from dormancy. And from the moment Uta, their leader, lays eyes on him, the die is cast. She sets her sights on winning the foreigner's heart and pours all her energy into showing him the best possible time during the rest of his stay in Paris. Her resolve is unbreakable. She is love-struck, and if Faust doesn't immediately feel the same, no matter. She'll wait it out.

Faust seems stunned by her attentions at first, not sure how to respond to her fluorescent hair, piercings, and tattoos. But her utter disregard of pretense finally wins him over. And by the end of the week, when she tells him she wants him to stay in Europe, he notifies Ava and me that he won't be returning with us.

Kate and Vincent. Charlotte and Ambrose. Uta and Faust. It's romance central at my Paris home—like Cupid packed up his quiver of arrows and moved into La Maison.

~

One morning, after studying maps of the Paris sewer systems side by side with diagrams of Manhattan subway, flood, and sewage tunnels, I notice Ava rubbing her eyes. "You okay?" I ask.

"Yeah, my eyes are just burning from focusing for so long," she says, raising her arms in a stretch and rolling her head from side to side.

"Have you seen the armory yet?" I ask.

"Only quickly when Kate gave me the house tour," she says. "But a workout is exactly what I could use right now."

"You should take advantage of having a European arms master at your disposal," I say, bumping Gaspard with my elbow.

Gaspard rolls up an ancient map that he had been showing us and shakes his head. "Any time I get away from helping America's new Champion strategize for a potential underground offensive against the numa, or, as Ambrose so charmingly dubbed it, 'Attack of the Mole People' . . ."

Ambrose fake-salutes and says, "Glad to contribute where I can."

". . . I need to help Charlotte with the wedding," Gaspard finishes.

Ambrose rubs his hands together. "I'm always up for a fight. I'll join you." He stands and stretches his arms, cracking his neck and bouncing up and down on his toes.

As the three of us make our way down to the armory, Ambrose quizzes Ava on the type of weapons used by American revenants, and she explains the gun/sword combo. "Besides swords, the only weapon we really use is modified bow and arrow."

"No crossbows? No battle-axes?" Ambrose asks. "How about scythes, maces, quarterstaffs?"

Ava shakes her head. "We have all sorts of specialized weapons in the Warehouse's armory, but I've never seen anyone use them. I wouldn't even know how to hold a few of them."

Ambrose rubs his hands. "Then you, my American sister, are in for a treat." I follow them down the stairs into the basement armory and show Ava where Kate and Charlotte keep their fighting gear. Ambrose rips off his shirt and pulls on a tight tank top over a pair of loose shorts. I would normally fight in just some drawstring karate pants, but I toss a soft gray T-shirt on top, knowing that Americans are a bit more sensitive to bared skin. And then I remember that Ava was a part of Warhol's Factory, and strip it back off.

Ambrose notices my wardrobe hesitation and winks. "You look better like that," he fake-whispers.

And then Ava walks out, and we're both rooted to the spot. Her hair is bundled up on the top of her head, and she wears the one-piece catsuit that Charlotte uses when there's a risk of getting sliced up.

Ambrose lets out a low whistle. "You are looking good, girl. And I'm saying that in a completely non-sleazy, I-love-my-fiancée kind of way." Ava looks pleased. Her gaze swings to me.

I hold up my hands. "I could say the same thing, but since I don't have a fiancée to hide potential sleaziness behind, I won't risk anything beyond, 'Why, Miss Whitefoot, you are looking extremely well today.'"

She bursts out laughing, and then, surveying my bare chest with a twinkle in her eye, says, "You are looking quite well yourself, Monsieur Marchenoir."

I give her a low bow. Ambrose moans. "Come on, guys. Let's get this fight on the road." And grabbing a quarterstaff from its pegs on the wall, he throws it to Ava, who catches it without batting an eye.

And for the next hour we spar, switching weapons from time

to time to change things up. Though Ava hasn't used most of them, she follows Ambrose's and my examples and quickly catches on. The three of us are fighting, sweating, quipping, teasing, laughing, and I can't remember the last time that I have felt so good.

⁓

That night at dinner, Ambrose takes a chair next to Charlotte and, putting his arm around her, nods toward me. "Check out Jules," he says.

"I know," she says, and lays her head on his shoulder.

"What?" I ask.

She grins at me. "You look almost happy."

Ava's eyes dart over to meet my own, and I feel my face redden. "Yeah, must be the fact that I'm back in Paris."

"Told you he missed us," Ambrose says, and pulls Charlotte to him in a powerful side-hug.

⁓

It is a beautiful wedding, held in the stained-glass jewel box that is La Sainte-Chapelle. Charlotte wears a vintage wedding gown from the 1940s, the era she was human. And Ambrose wears a custom-made tux, since not a shop in Paris had one big enough to fit him.

Charles has brushed his burgundy Mohawk down and even forgoes eyeliner in order to give his sister away. He is as radiant as the bride—his new life suits him well.

After blessing the wedding, the revenant priest steps aside and lets Gaspard officiate—which he does with a shaking voice and tears in his eyes. And when he says to kiss the bride, Ambrose lets out a whoop and swings Charlotte around before planting the kiss of the century on her rosy lips.

There isn't a dry eye in the house.

On my way out, I spot Arthur and Georgia sharing a private moment behind a column in the lower chapel. Kate had told me they were on-again, off-again. This must be an on day.

Back at La Maison, the reception is in full swing, with Faust and Uta hitting the dance floor before anyone else has their jackets off. He picks her up and flips her around in some kind of crazy swing number that I'd never imagined he could do. Faustino Molinaro is a never-ending surprise.

As the rest of the guests file into the ballroom, Ambrose lifts Charlotte up onto the dais and stands on the ground beneath her as she clinks her spoon on a champagne glass. She seems lit up from within: like there's a thousand-watt bulb beneath that creamy skin. This is everything she's ever wanted. For decades. The room falls silent, and everyone turns to face her.

"Ambrose and I said we weren't going to allow speeches. We've all known each other too long, and there are way too many incriminating stories that could surface."

Laughter rolls over the crowd, and winks and nudges are exchanged.

"But I just want to take a moment to thank everyone for being here today. Welcome, kindred. I especially want to thank the members of La Maison . . . my house. Gaspard, Jules, Vincent . . . and Ambrose. You were already here when Jean-Baptiste recovered Charles's and my bodies and invited us to stay. You have been my fathers, my brothers, my world. I have never known better men than you. And now I am marrying one of you."

"It's a done deal, baby," Ambrose remarks, looking up at her with a wink.

"Finally!" Charlotte teases, nudging his broad shoulder with her hip. Everyone laughs.

She lifts her glass. "Thank you for joining us on this day where our joy is truly complete. *Santé!*"

"Santé!" the crowd cheers, sipping their champagne in honor of the happy couple, and as the music starts back up, people crowd onto the dance floor. I look around for Ava, who I had only briefly glimpsed at the wedding, since I had to be there early and was seated in the front row with Vincent, Kate, Charles, and Jeanne. She must have been one of the first to leave the chapel, because I didn't see her afterward.

But now, there she is across the room, wearing a full-length ruby-colored gown, her hair pulled back into an elegant updo. She is stunning. My heart and throat do this simultaneous squeeze-and-choke thing, and I can't breathe for a full second. Which is one second too long, because some dashing guy from Geneviève's house steps in, gives her this gallant and totally annoying bow, and sweeps her onto the dance floor.

Chapter Fifteen

"How's your dance card look?" says the voice I know better than any other—it's been haunting my mind for months. And there is Kate, standing in front of me in her golden-auraed glory.

"Double-check your century, Kate," I respond. "And stop stealing my lines."

She gives me a sassy curtsy. I roll my eyes, and then, lunging, grab her around the waist and whisk her out onto the dance floor, making her laugh in delight.

"I've seen that dress before," I say of her Asian-print silk gown.

"It's my birthday dress," she replies.

"Ah, yes. The one Vincent had custom-made as a surprise for your sweet seventeenth."

"The very one," she says.

"That was a truly brilliant boyfriend move," I comment.

"Yeah," she says. "He's pretty good at those things."

We dance in silence for a moment, and then I say softly, "I hope you know how lucky you are. How lucky you both are."

She leans back to look at me, her face open with compassion. She doesn't need to say anything—we both know what the other is thinking. I measure the pain in my heart, and it is still there, but it is less. "I'm going to be okay," I say.

"I know," she replies, and lays her head on my shoulder. Other couples move around us, but for a few moments time stops and it's just the two of us, and my heart is calm and things are good.

And then Kate speaks and the magic is broken. "I've been spending a lot of time with Ava. She's pretty amazing, you know."

I stop and stare at her. "You're not going to try that old pass-the-guy-whose-heart-you-broke-onto-someone-else-so-you-won't-feel-guilty routine, are you? Because that is so beneath you."

"I wouldn't dream of it," Kate quips. She places her hands back on my shoulders and forces me to dance. "You're too smart for that."

"I accept that compliment and beg you to stop talking before you say anything else that could come across as pitying or demeaning."

"Deal," says Kate, and throws her arms around my neck. The song is ending, and she gives me a hug. "We're going to miss you," she says, and leaves me standing face-to-face with Ava, having craftily deposited me inches away.

I have no time to think. "Um, dance?" I ask.

"Lose your suave somewhere on the dance floor?" Ava asks, cracking a smile.

"Uh, yeah. I think Faust trampled it under those size twenties of his."

She laughs. "Let's go." She gives me her hand, and I lead her to a far corner of the room, away from the direction Kate wandered.

"You okay after that dance?" she asks, as I place one hand on her waist and grasp her hand in the other.

"Fighting form," I respond. She doesn't push the point, and I'm grateful that she doesn't want to Talk, with a capital *T*.

We dance for a moment, and I'm just beginning to realize that I've actually got Ava *in my arms* for the very first time. I'm starting to enjoy it . . . immensely, when she says something. I try to focus. "What?" I ask, and point at the speakers. "I can't hear you. The music . . ."

She moves her lips closer to my ear—I couldn't have planned it better if I'd tried. "I've seen the way you are with your kindred. They all love you. Respect you. You seem so at home here—you *are* at home here. Are you sure you want to come back to New York?"

Oh God. She does want to Talk. Please, not here. Not now. I hold her to me for one more moment and then pull back and tap my ear. "It really is too loud. Do you want to go somewhere else?" I say, hoping she'll just drop the whole subject.

"Yes."

I sigh. "Okay, follow me." I take her hand and weave through the crowd. We head toward the front door and step outside to see the garden crowded with guests. Georgia and Arthur are sitting on the edge of the fountain, bodies entwined and lips locked. God, do they ever give it a break?

"Back in," I say, and lead her up the winding front staircase, down the hallway past the library, and up the second set of stairs.

"Are we going to your room?" she asks.

"No. Better," I say, and passing my door, climb a few more steps and push open the trapdoor to the roof. It's pitch dark. I breathe a sigh of relief—no one else has had this idea—and I help her step out onto the dark roof before switching on the fairy lights.

"Oh, Jules!" she breathes, and raises her hands to her mouth, gazing around in wonder. Paris lies before us, lit up in all its nighttime magical glory. I smile. She's happy. I'm happy. If only it could last.

I open a cupboard near the door, pull out a few cushions and a blanket, and carry them over to a couch positioned at the edge of the roof that has the best view. "Milady?" I say, holding a hand out to her.

Speechless, she settles onto the couch, and I drape the blanket around her shoulders and sit down next to her.

"So . . . you were saying?"

She laughs, and takes a moment to reorganize her thoughts. "Right. Okay. I was saying . . . you seem so good here. Your kindred want you here. Are you sure you want to go back to New York tomorrow?"

"Yes, and I'm going to tell you why."

Ava watches me, head cocked to one side, waiting to hear what I have to say. My heartbeat accelerates under the scrutiny of her gaze. Should I? Shouldn't I? Should I . . . oh hell . . .

"I have a reason. You see, there's this girl."

"Girl?"

"Woman, rather, who I'm just getting to know. Who I would like to know better."

"What's she like?" Ava asks, a broad smile spreading across her lips.

"You're fishing!" I say, pointing at her and narrowing my eyes.

"Innocent curiosity, I swear." She makes the smile disappear and tries to look serious.

"Well, for one thing, she's drop-dead gorgeous and has the most interesting, unique look. A look that makes you want to keep on looking. Like your eyes are glued to her, and you can't rip them away."

"Ripping glued eyes, got it," she says.

"But I'm not the kind of guy who thinks that beauty's skin-deep. There's a lot more to her than meets the eye. You see, this girl's damaged"—Ava recoils slightly, and I put my hand up—

"like most people who have lived through traumatic events. But she's taken that pain and done something beautiful with it. She let it make her stronger. And people love her for that."

Ava just sits there, eyes wide, like she can't believe what she's hearing.

I drape my arm across the back of the couch and lean toward her. Here goes nothing. "Ava, I need you to know that this is very uncharacteristic of me . . . being this straightforward. But you have suffered in the past from someone deceiving you, so I am making it a point to be honest. Painfully so. The pain being all mine, I assure you." I exhale and massage my temples with my fingertips.

Ava shakes her head in awe. "I thought I knew you, before I even knew you . . . and it turns out I didn't know you at all."

"I'm not the same person I was before," I say, and I mean it. "I've changed."

Her gaze drops. "A broken heart can do that."

"Hearts mend," I say. "Especially when they have a good reason to."

Ava looks up and studies my face like it's one of her art books: like she's trying to see me from every possible angle, through all the layers into my core. Finally she tips her head and asks, "Are you saying that you like me, Jules Marchenoir?"

"I am saying that I like you very much indeed, Ava Whitefoot."

With a delighted grin, she crosses her arms and looks out over Paris.

I wait.

Are my palms actually sweating? I rub them on my pants and try not to think about what's going through her mind.

And then, with no warning, she leans forward, closes her eyes, and presses her lips to mine. My heart stops beating. She's kissing me. Ava is kissing me. My brain can't process what's happening, and my body responds automatically, arms circling her to draw her in toward me. She responds, placing her hands on my shoulders and running them down my arms, pushing them away, wriggling out of my grasp.

"No," she says, shaking her head, an amused smile on her lips. She leans forward and breathes next to my ear, "This is me. Let me."

I hold my hands up in surrender. "You, mademoiselle, are completely, one hundred percent, in control."

Her mouth quirks up on one side. "You don't know how good that sounds," she says, her words thick like honey. Then she takes my head in her hands and proceeds to electrify every inch of my body with the most perfect, warm, delicious kiss in the history of surprise rooftop kisses. No, I take that back . . . make that of any kiss ever. It's just long enough to turn my insides to jelly, but oh man, is it sweet.

"What was that for?" I ask, when I'm able to breathe again.

"It's a promise," she says, a playful twinkle in her eye.

"What's the promise?" I ask.

"That if you're good, you'll get some more."

"I don't think I've had such a compelling motivation in my life," I say, putting my hand on my heart in only half-joking earnestness.

"Then let's see how we do," Ava says.

She leans her head on my shoulder, and I wrap my arm around her, pulling her in close and keeping her there. Together, we look out over the lights of Paris, where, just beyond, is a wide, rolling countryside that ends at an ocean. And on the other side of that ocean lies a bright, shining city of dreams. A city of promise.

Epilogue

I'm in my room in the Warehouse, lacing up my steel-toed boots, when there's a knock on the door. "It's open," I yell, and Theodore Gold walks in, dressed in a black tuxedo. Black. Not white. I barely recognize him.

"Don't tell me you're going to fight in that," I say. "It looks like you just came from having dinner with the mayor."

"Funnily enough, I did just come from dinner with the mayor, and yes, I am fighting in this. I happen to find wool blend surprisingly comfortable in battle."

I can't tell if he's joking until he undoes a couple of pearl buttons to show the Kevlar vest he's wearing underneath.

I shrug. "Suit yourself, you've been in this game longer than I have." I strap the weapon belt around the waist of my leather jeans and, reaching for my own Kevlar vest, ease it over my black T-shirt.

Gold thrusts his hands in his pockets and does his strolling thing around my room. "I haven't been in here since your trip to Paris. What would that be . . . six months ago? I must say . . . I approve of the change in decor." He points up to a life-size portrait of Ava hanging on my wall. In it, she sits on a couch on a rooftop in a crimson evening gown, looking out over a moonlit Paris.

I snap the vest up the side. "It seems I've got myself a new muse."

"Yes, well," he says, trying to suppress a grin, "I'm actually not here to browse your newest works. I come as a messenger. You've got visitors. In the armory."

I pull on a lightweight chain-mail shirt and top it with a long-sleeved black jersey. "Visitors?" I ask, slipping my Glock and sword into their holsters. I pat myself down, verifying I've got everything, then grab my leather jacket. Gold holds the door open for me, and we head out into the hallway toward the stairs.

"I actually put a call out to a few other areas, since this skirmish has the potential of escalating into all-out war," he says. We follow other black-garbed kindred down the stairway and emerge through industrial metal doors into the Warehouse's lower level.

We take a quick right into the gym-size armory, and there he is, standing in the middle of the room, swinging around a massive battle-ax like it's a child's aluminum baton. My heart skips a beat. It's Ambrose. Here. In New York. "Lightweight American play toys," I hear him grumble, and then he sees me. Dropping the ax, he charges over and tackles me, nearly picking me up off my feet with his bear hug.

"What are you doing here?" I manage to squeak.

"Thanks to Gold, we heard about the big skirmish going down in Queens tonight. Since you yourself seem to be so . . . communication challenged."

"Yeah, sorry about that. I've been a bit busy." I turn, hearing a familiar squeal coming from the changing room.

Charlotte, dressed in battle gear, hurls herself across the room toward me and leaps into my arms. Dropping back to the ground, she kisses my cheeks and says, "Shame on you for not telling us about the battle. Ambrose has been going stir-crazy in Paris. He says there's no more action in France."

"Kate, Vincent, and Arthur wanted to come, but Gaspard insisted that it would be the perfect opportunity for a surprise attack from any numa 'stragglers,'" Ambrose says, using air quotes.

"So we brought a dozen of Paris's bardia with us," Charlotte says. "Everyone's suited up and ready to fight."

"I'm glad you came," I say, not quite believing that they're standing there with me, an ocean away from where they're supposed to be—safe behind the walls of La Maison.

The room has been emptying as we talk, and Gold slips out without saying good-bye. I hear the door open, and from behind me comes a voice. Her voice.

"Are you guys going to stand around all night chatting, or are you ready to fight?" Ava strides into the room, looking like a Hollywood costume designer's vampire-hunting dream girl: tight black leather, faux-fur vest, knee-high Doc Martens, and some serious metal strapped to chest, back, and waist.

I try to swallow, but it seems there's a baseball lodged inside my throat.

Ambrose whistles and Charlotte grins. Ava walks up to us. I clear my throat and say, "Although you've already met, I'd like to present to you Ava Whitefoot"—I get down on one knee and hold my hand up to her—"Champion of my heart, as well as of the American Eastern Seaboard."

Ava laughs and takes the hand I'm offering. "That started out romantic and then kind of fizzled out at the end."

"Yeah, I've got to work on downplaying the literalism," I say, and allow her to lift me from my courtly position before grabbing her and pulling her to me for a five-second heart-thumping kiss.

"Watch the blades," Ambrose suggests, "or this could go down as most dangerous make-out session ever."

"Worth it," I say, letting go of her with a twinge of regret.

"If we win," Ava murmurs, with a twinkle in her eye, "there will be more later."

"Then let's go slay some numa!" I grab her hand and lead the group out of the armory, down a hallway, and into a parking garage that holds a veritable army of vehicles. Next to each car, a small group of kindred stands at the ready, dressed for battle and armed to the teeth. There must be close to two hundred bardia assembled in this one room.

"No. Way," breathes Ambrose, taking in the scene before us. He turns to Charlotte. "We're moving here." She laughs and rolls her eyes.

"Jules?" Ava asks, and I put my fingers to my lips and let out a sharp whistle. The room falls silent, and all eyes turn to where we stand at the top of the stairs leading down into the garage.

"Our strategy is solid," Ava says, her voice echoing through the vast hall. "And from what I can see, we will easily outnumber the numa group assembled. We are ready for this battle. A victory tonight will mean a lethal blow to their infrastructure. Come fight with me, kindred."

She unsheathes her sword and swings it in a slow arc across the room, meeting every person's eye before lifting her sword toward the ceiling and saying in a slow and steady voice, "Let's. Do. This."

The place goes berserk, two hundred bardia cheering and hugging and high-fiving like they've already won. Ambrose stares at Ava, gobsmacked, while a proud smile stretches across Charlotte's lips. She leans over to Ava and yells over the noise. "You are *amazing*!"

Ava smiles broadly and nods to me. I give another whistle, and people jump into their cars, SUVs, and motorcycles, and begin pulling out of the garage and onto the Brooklyn streets.

She takes my hand as we make our way down the stairs into the room and toward a waiting car. *Merci, mon chevalier,* she says in my head, and leans in toward me for one last prebattle kiss.

I oblige, cradling her head in my hands, and let my lips express what my heart cannot say: that I am hers, body and soul. And when we finally part, she smiles in that way that makes me know I've found my true home.

My home is not a place. It's not a fixed location on the map; not Paris or New York. It is with Ava. Wherever she is—that is where I belong. I look at her and my heart is full. I respond, "You are welcome, *mon coeur.*"

About Amy Plum

Amy Plum is the international bestselling author of young adult novels, including the DIE FOR ME, AFTER THE END, and DREAMFALL series. Her books have been translated into thirteen languages. Amy grew up in Birmingham, Alabama before venturing further afield to Chicago, Paris, London and New York. An art historian by training, she can be found on most days either daydreaming or writing (or both) in a Paris café.

Die for Her

Set in the romantic and death-defying world of the international bestselling *Die for Me* series, this original novella follows Jules, a brooding, immortal French artist who has fallen in love with his best friend's girlfriend.

Jules Marchenoir is a revenant—an undead being whose fate forces him to sacrifice himself over and over again to save human lives. He's spent the better part of the last century flirting his way through Paris, but when he met Kate Mercier, the heroine from Amy Plum's Die for Me series, he knew his afterlife had changed forever and he had found the love of his life. Until Kate fell for his best friend, Vincent. Now Jules is faced with an impossible decision: choosing between his loyal friend and a love truly worth dying for.

Chapter One

The first time I see her, I peg her as a jump risk.

Vince and I are walking the quays, and there she is: long, dark hair whipping around her face as she stands on the edge of the cobblestone walkway looking down at the water, a mere five feet above the waves. The Seine is swollen from winter rains, so though the jump would be harmless from that height, the barely choppy surface could hide dangerous currents.

We head toward her, my hand already extended to touch her arm. To pass my calm to her, one of our only real "superpowers" as a revenant (or, as Ambrose likes to call us, "undead guardian angels with a bad case of OCD"). But before we reach her she turns and walks away, heading for one of the quay's stone benches, where she curls her legs up to her chest and ropes her knees in with her arms. She remains that way, hugging herself, rocking back and forth, and staring blindly across the river with tears coursing down her cheeks, as we pass unnoticed.

"What do you think?" I ask Vincent, who pulls his scarf up over his nose and mouth, shielding himself from the frigid January wind.

"I don't think she's going to jump," he says. "But let's circle around under the bridge to make sure."

We stride side by side until we get to the Carrousel Bridge. Even the indigents who regularly sleep under its arches have cleared out. It is one of the coldest days on record . . . at least since I moved to Paris a century ago.

We good revenants, called *bardia*, are fated to watch over humans, saving them from premature death by suicide, murder, or accident. Our job is definitely easier in weather like this, with everyone staying indoors. But even members of the reanimated undead can feel the cold.

Most of our work for the last few days has been rounding up the few remaining street people and getting them to care centers before they suffer frostbite or even death from exposure. Judging by her clothes and hygiene, this girl is definitely not homeless. Instead she's pretty enough to add to my girls-to-ask-out list. However, hitting on someone who is crying isn't quite my style.

So if she's not homeless, why is she here, taking a solitary stroll next to the river in the freezing cold?

We confirm that there are no stragglers under the bridge, and then turn to head back to the bench. When we reach it, it is empty. A few yards away, I see the girl climbing the stairs to street level. Since there's no one else around, we follow her at a safe distance, ready to run if she heads for the bridge. "Ambrose, use your foresight—do you see her jumping?" I ask.

Naw. The word skips my ears and goes straight to my mind in Ambrose's deep baritone. *But she* is *about to sprint up the rue du Bac.*

"We should follow her," I say to Vincent. "She's acting bizarrely enough to merit a few more minutes of surveillance."

"Agreed. She could still throw herself in front of a car," he says, concerned. "Something's obviously wrong with her."

"I'm banking on it being the result of a bad breakup," I reply. "That's what happens when people get too serious. Feelings get hurt. Hearts get broken. Some people never learn. Don't get serious. It's my number one rule." I rub my hands together and blow on them, trying to force hot breath through my wool gloves. "My fingers are icicles. And the streets are empty. Let's head back to La Maison."

Wimp, taunts Ambrose.

"Hey, if you weren't currently disembodied, you'd be agreeing with me, ghost boy," I say, and hear him chuckle. Vincent isn't paying attention and picks up his pace. I glance ahead of us and see that the girl has started to run.

We follow her, leaving a good half block between us: There is no traffic for her to throw herself in front of, and we don't want to call unnecessary attention to ourselves. She jogs up the rue du Bac, crosses the boulevard Saint-Germain, and finally turns left at a square where old, stately apartment buildings are grouped around a small park.

She walks up to one, and while opening the door, turns and casts a quick look behind her. Vincent and I duck our heads down and walk straight up the rue du Bac without her seeing our faces.

But I saw hers. And her expression is one I recognize—I've seen it many times during my existence. Especially in the line of "work" I'm in. The girl is suffering from terrible grief.

Vincent and I lock eyes, and I tip my head left. Toward home. He understands and we walk to the end of the block, turning eastward toward La Maison. It's not like we can read each other's minds. But when you're best friends with someone for over half a century, you start to recognize their every gesture. We're like an old couple. Words are almost unnecessary.

We walk for a while in silence, keeping an eye out for anything amiss. Ambrose doesn't spot any activity at all in the neighborhood and is singing a Louis Armstrong song directly into my brain, probably to piss me off. "Who is the lucky lady tonight?" Vincent asks as he taps the code into our security panel. The gate swings slowly open.

"Quintana," I respond.

"From?"

"New York, upstate somewhere. Over here doing an art degree."

"Blond?" he asks.

"Negative," I respond. "Dark hair with blue tips. Alternative chic."

"Sounds like your type," he jokes. We both know I don't have a type. "Female" is my type.

Like I said. We're an old couple—we need few words. But we couldn't be more different. Vincent stopped dating decades ago, not that he had been much into it before. "What's the point?" he had said. This was around 1980, and that year's bouquet of Parisiennes was breathtaking.

"What's the *point*?" I exclaimed. "They're beautiful. And soft. And they smell good. What do you mean, 'what's the point'?"

"We can only go so far, and then we have to disappear from their lives. It's not worth it if we can't even get close," he sighed.

"Excuse me, but I make it a regular habit of 'getting close'!"

"I don't mean like that," he responded. "I'm talking *emotional* intimacy. And why risk exposure of our entire kindred for a girl you're only going to spend a few nights with?" His expression was flat. Uncaring. But I knew there was an ocean of pain bottled inside him.

"Man, no one will ever compare to Hélène. It's been seventy years since you saw her murdered by those Nazis and you're still hanging on. You've just got to accept that your first love is your greatest, and everything else is going to be second-best. But second-best is better than nothing at all."

My arguments fall on deaf ears with Vincent. If he won't amuse himself with humans, the only other choice is to go revenant. And we know pretty much all of the female members of our kindred in France. They're like sisters to us. Revenants do occasionally fall for one another. It happens. But it just hasn't happened to Vincent or me. And until the next global convocation, we probably won't meet any new *bardia* beauties.

Which is A-OK with me. Why settle for one girl if you can have a lot? It's a good motto, I find. Works for drinks, friends, and women. Not so much for enemies. But our situation in France is stable. Similar number of numa and *bardia*. The balance of good and evil has reached an equilibrium in the past few years.

Which means I've got time to play.

Printed in Great Britain
by Amazon